KU-637-425

About Aimee Carson

The summer she turned eleven, Aimee left the children's section of the library and entered an aisle full of Harlequin Mills & Boon® novels. She promptly pulled out a book, sat on the floor, and read the entire story. It has been a love affair that has lasted for over thirty years.

Despite a fantastic job working part-time as a physician in the Alaskan Bush (think *Northern Exposure* and *ER*, minus the beautiful mountains and George Clooney), she also enjoys being at home in the gorgeous Black Hills of South Dakota, riding her dirt bike with her three wonderful kids and beyond patient husband. But, whether at home or at work, every morning is spent creating the stories she loves so much. Her motto? Life is too short to do anything less than what you absolutely love. She counts herself lucky to have two jobs she adores, and incredibly blessed to be a part of Harlequin Mills & Boon's family of talented authors.

™

Praise for Aimee Carson

'Oh, my, what a fantastic debut by Aimee Carson.
I loved it! It really has everything that I like
in a good contemporary romance: a feisty heroine
who is far from perfect, snappy dialogue and
sizzling chemistry—and I mean sizzling. *That* scene
in the elevator...*phew*! The romance and relationship
between Alyssa and Paulo is actually quite simple, but
perfectly done. Aimee's writing flows beautifully, and
she has created two great characters. I applaud her for
Alyssa's "bad girl" roots, I loved her! The book is well
written and developed, with plenty of sass and sparkle.
I can't wait to read more from Aimee in the future.'
—www.everyday-is-the-same.blogspot.com on
Secret History of a Good Girl

First Time
For Everything

Aimee Carson

MILLS & BOON

All the characters in this book have no existence outside the imagination of the author, and have no relation whatsoever to anyone bearing the same name or names. They are not even distantly inspired by any individual known or unknown to the author, and all the incidents are pure invention.

All Rights Reserved including the right of reproduction in whole or in part in any form. This edition is published by arrangement with Harlequin Enterprises II BV/S.à.r.l. The text of this publication or any part thereof may not be reproduced or transmitted in any form or by any means, electronic or mechanical, including photocopying, recording, storage in an information retrieval system, or otherwise, without the written permission of the publisher.

® and TM are trademarks owned and used by the trademark owner and/or its licensee. Trademarks marked with ® are registered with the United Kingdom Patent Office and/or the Office for Harmonisation in the Internal Market and in other countries.

First published in Great Britain 2013
by Mills & Boon, an imprint of Harlequin (UK) Limited.
Harlequin (UK) Limited, Eton House, 18-24 Paradise Road,
Richmond, Surrey TW9 1SR

© Aimee Carson 2013

ISBN: 978 0 263 23436 7

MORAY COUNCIL LIBRARIES & INFO.SERVICES		
20 35 28 14		
Askews & Holts		ewable
		tainable
RF RF		the

Also by Aimee Carson

Secret History of a Good Girl
How to Win the Dating War
Dare She Kiss & Tell?
The Best Mistake of Her Life

Did you know these are also available as eBooks?
Visit www.millsandboon.co.uk

™

Jacqueline "Jax" Lee, my heroine in this story,
constantly amazed me with her indomitable spirit
and quirky sense of humor. So it's only fitting that
I dedicate this book to two of the strongest, funniest
women I know: Wendy S. Marcus and Jennifer Probst.
Not only are you both fabulous authors and
my soul sisters, y'all somehow manage to keep me sane.
I love you both.

CHAPTER ONE

RAY-BAN SUNGLASSES blocking the bright sun, Blake Bennington made his way down the courthouse steps, debating whether to ask Sara out before getting back to the office. Regardless of his decision, his fourteen-hour workday would have to be cut short for his appearance at the annual Moon Over Miami fundraiser tonight. Which meant, after ten hours in a tie, he was destined to trade his suit for a tux. But the discomfort would be a small price to pay given his sister Nikki's involvement with the event was what had kept her out of trouble since her arrival back home.

Blake pushed the troublesome thoughts aside. "Thanks for the info, Sara."

Beside him, the striking brunette in a power suit sent him a smile laced with a subtle come-hither vibe. Blake had been studiously sidestepping her interest since the first time they'd collaborated on the South Florida Drug Enforcement Task Force, years ago.

"Winning a guilty verdict in the Menendez case will solidify your chances for promotion, Blake," she said. "I hope the file helps."

"Every piece of information helps." They reached the busy sidewalk and he stopped to face the beautiful lawyer. "Seriously," he said. "I appreciate your time."

"You know I'm always available," Sara said as she brushed his arm with her fingers, and Blake bit back a smile.

Her touch seemed like a simple gesture, but he knew better.

Sara was classy. Poised. And intelligent. Known for being a bulldog in the courtroom, she possessed a dedication and pragmatism that rivaled his. Just the sort of woman Blake should date. Just the sort of woman Blake usually *did* date. One who understood his career goals and the time requirements.

So why was he hesitating?

While the question darted around his head, a passing lawyer stopped to ask Sara a question, and Blake paused, knowing he was a fool for ignoring the offer in her eyes. Nikki might be more of a time-consuming handful than a little sister had a right to be, not to mention the high-profile case that currently required his full attention, but he was a red-blooded man who enjoyed sex as much as the next guy. Despite ample opportunity, it had been six months since he'd last woken up with a woman in his bed. Six months since he'd followed through on the urge.

What was his problem?

As he contemplated the question, a female who looked barely old enough to vote plowed into him, her eyes fixed on her phone as one of her black-booted heels landed on his toes. Gripping her arms, Blake stared down at the long, honey-colored hair, the Beatles T-shirt and the enticing cutoffs—not short enough to reveal the underwear beneath, but coming pretty damn close. His internal debate made a lateral move from his sex life to whether there was lace or a thong beneath the shorts. And combined with the sight of sexy leather cowboy boots…

Man, he seriously needed to get a grip.

His feminine assailant slipped her phone into her pocket and removed her foot from his. "Sorry, Suit," she drawled, and Blake set her back, his eyebrows pulling together in amusement at the nickname. "I'm running late," she went on, "but that's no excuse for body-slamming you."

"You should watch where you're going," he said lightly. He nodded down at the fantasy-inducing footwear. "With boots like those, someone might get hurt."

"Cheer up. Maybe you can successfully sue me for a hit-and-run."

The infectious sparkle in her hazel eyes was more humor than seduction.

"Except you haven't run," he said, attempting to maintain a serious expression, knowing he was failing. "And technically, if you left me your name, I'd have no case."

"Well, when you put it like that..." She stuck out her hand, and Blake took it automatically, noting the soft skin and the small tattoo on the inside of her wrist. "Jacqueline Lee," she said. "And just in case you were considering asking me out—" she released his hand "—everyone calls me Jax."

Blake realized his previous words had been misconstrued as a come-on, and his forehead bunched in skeptical humor. "I don't date jailbait."

"I'm twenty-three and of sound mind and body," she said. He didn't know her well enough to verify the state of her mind, but it was obvious her body was most definitely sound. She tilted her head. "Does that help?"

He lifted an eyebrow in amusement. "It would, except I never date a woman who goes by a man's name."

Her wide smile at his fictitious—and ridiculous—dating guideline was alluring. "That's an awful lot of rules you got there," she said. She turned to go and then paused, shooting him a mischievous look over her shoulder. "Give me a call when you want to break one."

An amused scoff of doubt escaped as he watched her head out onto the courthouse lawn. When was the last time he'd engaged in a harmless flirtation? Too long, apparently. It was definitely time for him to start dating again if he was noticing a little hellion on heels. Hardly the kind of woman he needed in his life.

An old V W Beetle parked in front of the courthouse began to blast a song loud enough to fill the bustling courthouse lawn. And one minute his sexy assailant was crossing the grassy grounds, the next she was stepping out into a dance routine. Stunned, Blake struggled to make sense of her actions until, one by one, she was joined by adolescents in a clearly choreographed routine. Soon, more than a dozen youth were engaged in a dance number good enough to be aired on a professional music video.

"Oh, for heaven's sake, a flash mob," Sara said as she came to a stop beside him. Her voice was loaded with disapproval. "Don't kids these days have anything better to do?"

Blake stared at the group and, in particular, their leader, passion oozing from her every movement. Her earlier playful tone couldn't be taken seriously, but the earnest enthusiasm on her face now was mesmerizing.

"They're just having fun, Sara," he said with a distracted tone.

There was a time when he used to live to have fun, having entirely too much of it along the way. But just because he'd crashed headfirst into reality when his father had died, leaving the responsibility for his madcap family on Blake's shoulders, that didn't mean the rest of the world needed one of life's hardest lessons at the age of twenty.

"No harm in that," he went on.

There was harm, however, in the way he was appreciating the fluid movements of the hazel-eyed girl/woman. She twisted, twirled and moved to the Latino hip-hop song—an odd choice given her cowboy boots—with a supple grace that was capable of contorting her body into almost impossible positions. Her dancing fired his imagination, turning his blood to molten metal.

"No harm? Tell that to the police. They don't look amused at all," Sara said. "They look ready to make an arrest."

With effort, Blake shifted his gaze to the two unsmiling cops rapidly approaching the dance group, his mind filling with an interesting image of his hit-and-run perpetrator in handcuffs. And *not* in a professional capacity.

What the hell was wrong with him?

Blake gazed at the aforementioned policemen as one of them stopped to address the dancers engaged in the routine— a routine that currently involved undulating on the grass in an impressive dance move—while the other cop made a beeline for the beat-up VW Beetle blaring the music. And, for the first time, Blake noticed the leg encased in a long cast sticking out from the passenger seat of the offending car.

A weary groan of frustration escaped his lips, and his entertainment in the scene came to a screeching halt.

There was no doubt in his mind who the leg belonged to, because it was highly unlikely there could be *two* casts in Miami emblazoned with a red dragon from hip to toes. A cast tattoo, his sister had called it.

Hand on the VW's hood, the police officer hunched over to speak with the hidden occupant, the cast engulfing the leg like a plaster anchor. One that Blake had thought would keep Nikki from landing in hot water—like getting thrown in jail. At least until he'd wrapped up his current case.

And there was nothing Blake hated more than being wrong.

Six hours later

"I came to arrange your release from jail as a favor to my sister, Ms. Lee," Blake Bennington said, and Jax winced, saying a prayer of thanks, *again*, that she'd been the only one arrested today. The black interior of the limo and the lawyer's dark good looks were a sharp contrast to his cool gray eyes as he went on. "Arguing the merits of the Miami Police Department with you wasn't part of the deal."

Beside him, Jax squirmed against the plush leather seat. Calling her new friend, Nikki Bennington, for advice had seemed logical. When the law student had shared that her brother was less than amused by today's escapades, Jax couldn't have cared less about some unknown stuffed shirt. Until she'd learned that Nikki's deal with her brother meant he'd informed his chauffer to bypass a charity event and head for the jail to help. Before Blake Bennington had arrived, Jax had vowed to honor the generous gesture by holding her tongue to keep the peace.

A peace that had been most profoundly disturbed.

The hairs on her arms still stood on end from the initial electrifying sight of her hit-and-run victim materializing to offer assistance. After hours in custody, she should have been too spent to feel anything. But it wasn't every day a girl was rescued from behind bars by a tuxedo-clad man more gorgeous than James Bond...leaving her body both shaken *and* stirred.

"I wasn't arguing the police department's merits," she said, trying again for a conciliatory tone, which was pathetic at best. "I was just..." She forced herself to meet his gaze, the now familiar imposing form creating a jolting sizzle.

The attraction was horribly inconvenient, especially with the disapproving vibes he exuded. Keeping her opinions to herself wasn't her usual style, and much, *much* harder than she'd originally thought.

She hiked her chin, aiming to bring a diplomatic end to their debate. "I was just questioning their priorities."

Blake tipped his head. "And I'm sure the police would love to accommodate you and your priorities," he said smoothly, clearly not meaning the words. "But they have a job to do and are bound by the letter of the law. So for future reference—" a single brow lifted, a perfect match to his wry tone "—disturbing the peace, no matter how innocently it's done, is illegal."

Jax bit her tongue at his tone, reminding herself to think of Nikki. *Think of Nikki.* During their previous run-in, Blake had appeared approachable, almost relaxed, but the moment he'd shown up to arrange her release, his intense lawyerly attitude had shown up, as well. Yet through it all the man had remained so cool. So calm. And now he was so right, damn him.

One more statement pleading her point of view and then she'd happily remain silent. "I didn't plan this event with the intention of breaking the law."

As if preparing for an interesting story, Blake leaned back, his posture one of a man in control. One arm thrown along the seat behind her. One leg crossed over the other. And two eyes focused on her as if daring her to impress him with her explanation.

"Then what was your intention?" he said.

"I work as a music therapist at South Glade Teen Center, an after-school club for kids. The county pulled their funding…"

Her heart rate jumped, fear squeezing her chest. The club provided a safe place for the kids to be themselves. To *belong.* Without the facility, her high school years would have been unbearable. Shifting from foster family to foster family, South Glade had been the only constant, the one place she'd truly felt at home. Losing it now wasn't an option.

Seeking calm, she rubbed the small tattoo that partially disguised the two well-healed scars on her wrist. Warrior wounds, she liked to call them. Symbols of her past. They reminded her of who she was.

And how far she'd come.

She straightened her shoulders and pushed the panic aside. "So I wanted to gain a little positive publicity for our cause."

"By getting arrested?"

Was he mocking her?

She inhaled a soothing breath, straining for patience.

"That's how Nikki got involved. A mutual friend asked her for tips on how to proceed legally."

And you should have followed Nikki's advice more closely, Jax.

Blake appeared unimpressed with her explanation. "Well, according to the police report, the music blaring from your VW Beetle was loud enough to disturb the peace."

Inwardly, she winced, hating her defensive tone. "I told Nikki it's kinda hard to keep the beat to music you can't hear."

He went on as if she hadn't spoken. "Not to mention the dance move that landed you on the sidewalk where you—" he leaned forward to the seat across from them and retrieved the report, scanning the page "—and I quote…'failed to comply with a lawful order to cease from obstructing a public sidewalk.' End quote."

His gaze landed on hers again, and heat crept up her face, but she refused to let him see her blush. So Jax concentrated very hard on brushing away the grains of sand clinging to her denim cutoffs, remnants of her time spent on the ground.

"I couldn't hear the police officer's order to move because of the music," she mumbled.

"Precisely," he said evenly.

She shot him a look she hoped was veiled by her lashes, her voice growing stronger. "And I didn't intend to land on the sidewalk. I just overshot my mark doing the Worm."

He raised a brow higher. "I assume you're referring to the dance step that involved you undulating along the ground on your belly."

He set the report on the seat between them and went still, as if he couldn't *wait* for her to explain further. Somehow she didn't think further details would help.

"The maneuver isn't easy to do," she said.

"It certainly looked painful."

She ignored him and went on. "And I unintentionally positioned myself in the wrong spot. I didn't know that I was getting too close to the walkway."

"In retrospect, a fatal error in judgment," he said drily.

The sarcasm was really getting on her nerves.

"There was no time to practice," she said. "We needed to react quickly to the budget cuts. While the news was fresh in the public's mind."

He settled a little deeper into the seat. "And you thought taking the teens you were responsible for out on a flash mob and risking arrest was a good expression of your dissatisfaction?"

Jeez, putting it like that made her feel like a crazy lady. "I told you, I was *trying* to keep it legal."

Above the pristine tux and the tanned, flawless complexion of his face, the two dark slashes of eyebrows were perfectly schooled into a noncommittal expression. And despite the sophisticated polish and the undertones of skepticism, she suddenly got the impression that Blake Bennington was as amused as he was disapproving of her actions.

She narrowed her eyes suspiciously. "Deep down, you find this whole thing funny, don't you?"

"Just the part where your carefully planned flash mob was ruined by a dance move." His lips twitched, as if suppressing a grin. "Perhaps next time you'll plan your routine more carefully."

The hint of restrained humor was annoying, and she said, "And perhaps Officer Brown will learn to lighten up a little?"

His eyebrows shot higher as the gray eyes grew dark, holding her in their power as he leaned closer. She'd obviously stepped on a nerve.

"I can assure you, Ms. Lee. When it comes to people who break the law—" his voice was deadly soft, and his proximity brought her attraction back in full force "—both Officer Brown and I take our jobs very seriously."

Trapped by the force of his gaze, Jax's heart rapped harder

beneath her ribs. Getting beyond the thickly fringed, hyp-notizing eyes was difficult, but she finally allowed her gaze to skim down the angular planes of his face, landing on his mouth.

Oh, *great*...he had lips just the way she liked them. Full. Sensual. The kind that could kiss a girl senseless and make her forget she'd sworn off men forever. Or at least until she found one who *didn't* think she was certifiable.

And Superman here, with the eyes of steel, clearly wasn't the type.

As their staring contest continued, another heated flush slowly crept up her face, but she refused to feel ashamed. Because regret would keep her tethered to the past, unable to move on.

Relying on an innocent expression to tone down her state-ment, she said, "Are you lecturing me?" She lightly scrunched up her face, as if she didn't already know the answer. "Be-cause this is beginning to feel a lot like a lecture."

Amazingly, his lips twitched. "Not at all. But since you now have several charges filed against you requiring your attention, you should learn to follow advice."

Advice? Pressing her lips together, Jax turned her gaze to the window, drumming her fingers against the leather seat. Advice seemed a tame description for 007's fetish for con-trol. Not to mention those disturbing shoulders that were so broad you'd need a map to kiss your way from one side to the other...

Shoulders currently encased in a tuxedo—a blatant re-minder of how he'd sacrificed his plans to help her out, and here she was taking issue with his every word. She curled her hand into a fist.

Oh, perfect—*guilt*. Just what she didn't need.

She let out a sigh. "Look, I know you had plans." She took in the strong, stubble-free jaw and the crisp, horizontal precision of his black bow tie. "And I'm sorry I ruined your evening."

The look he gave her revealed little. "That's debatable."

"Debatable I'm *sorry* or that I ruined your evening?"

His forehead crinkled in suppressed humor. "I can't attest to your capacity for remorse. But rest assured..." He paused before going on, the lines fading from his brow. "It was a dinner function I was happy to miss."

"Then why were you going?"

His tone grew vague, as if briefly stumped by the question. "Responsibilities, Ms. Lee."

Curious, Jax paused. The air conditioner kicked on, and cold air hit. Her tank top and cutoffs, perfect for a flash dance mob under the Florida sun, now left her feeling exposed. And next to the sinfully sexy lawyer and his limousine of luxury, she felt positively scruffy. Tugging on her frayed hem, she tried to cover more skin. It was hopeless, so Jax resorted to rubbing her arms to overcome the chill.

Blake glanced at her and then flipped the AC switch, cutting off the blast of air. "Next time you plan on risking arrest, maybe you should choose a more suitable outfit."

She suppressed a groan. "Can we just agree it wasn't my *finest* moment and leave it at that?"

"Since I've just met you, I'll have to take you at your word." His gaze drifted down to her chest, and the ever-present tension expanded to a level that made the air crackle like the night sky over Times Square on New Year's Eve. Heat filled her gut as her heart thumped loudly in response, and she prayed her body wouldn't betray her attraction.

He lifted his hand to point at her tank top. "And you still have some mud from that less-than-fine moment stuck to Paul McCartney's face."

Startled, Jax glanced down. A light brown streak was smeared across her tank top emblazoned with the Fab Four. Paul's forehead covered her left breast and was smudged in a golden-brown color. Humiliation flared as she repeatedly swiped at the spot with trembling fingers, her bracelets tinkling. She knew Blake was watching her, and the tight knot of desire grew. Until her breasts gave her up, the tips pebbling.

"I'm afraid you're only making it worse," he said, his rumbling voice tinged with an unidentifiable emotion.

She gritted her teeth, and her bracelets continued their musical sound as she rubbed harder. Please, God, let him be referring to the smudge she'd smeared bigger with her efforts.

Blake leaned forward to shed his coat, his white shirt pulling tight against a wall of muscle that short-circuited her brain. Which was the only reason she dumbly let him slip the jacket around her shoulders.

It was warm. Heavy. With a seductive scent of a fresh sea breeze. Enveloping her like an embrace…

Oh, *heck*, no. "I'm fine, thank you," she said with a tight smile, and lifted her hand to remove the jacket.

His fingers encircled her wrist, stopping her movements, and the skin-on-skin contact sent a wave of heat up her cheeks.

"Quit being stubborn." His usual gray gaze had gone slate, his voice low. "You're cold, so leave it."

Flickers of electrical energy continued to skitter out in concentric circles from his touch, until Blake released her wrist to unbutton his cuffs and push up his sleeves. As if he wouldn't allow further debate.

Brother of her new friend or not, his attitude was hard to take.

"Look," she said as patiently as she could, "I know I'm not the kind of woman you typically associate with, but—"

"You haven't known me long enough to determine the kind of women I associate with," he said without looking at her.

Jax let out a quiet grunt. "Time enough to know all I need," she muttered.

He lifted his gaze to hers. "That's highly unlikely."

Every muscle in her body tensed. There it was again. The same überconfident, master-of-all-he-surveyed look. And right then and there she realized that even *attempting* to keep the peace was no longer an option.

She folded her arms tight across her chest. "Shall I tell you what I think?"

Leaning back, he studied her carefully. "You appear committed to sharing your every thought," he said, his voice now laced with amusement. "Why stop now?"

His tone pricked a nerve. Without a doubt, it was time she provided him and that God complex of his with a much-needed reality check. Anticipation soaring, Jax twisted in her seat to face him.

"You choose your clothes to impress." She paused, remembering the restrained impatience as he'd shoved up his sleeves. "Not necessarily because you like them, but as a symbol of your success. To convince the masses you're good at—" She crinkled her brow. "What exactly do you do?"

"I'm an assistant U.S. attorney."

"Impressive." She avoided the cool eyes watching her expectantly. "You wear your hair conservatively short, but leave it longer on top to avoid looking too militant." Her fingers itched to dig into thick waves and muss them up, just to see what he'd do. "What are you? Thirty? Thirty-one?"

"Thirty-two."

So nine years, numerous tax brackets and an alternate reality separated them.

She briefly inspected the deliciously bared forearms lined with muscle and sinew, irritated that his lethal sensuality was so utterly intoxicating. She avoided the tall, dark and disturbingly intense type, but this man had the heat rising in her body like hot oil in a lava lamp.

And the reemergence of a sense of humor made him vastly more appealing.

"I'd bet big money those muscles are courtesy of your

home gym equipment and not from a love of sports." From the look on his face, she knew she was right. "You keep in shape as part of your image. The self-discipline thing and all that," she said with a dismissive wave of her hand, her bracelets tinkling again.

"An art you obviously don't subscribe to," he said, his level gaze not budging.

"In relationships you prefer women like yourself." Biting back a smile, she went on, ignoring his dig. "Rules number one and two state they must be sensible and practical."

"Wrong." He leaned closer, bringing the gray eyes into sharper focus, and the breath stalled in her throat as her head spun from his towering proximity. "Those are numbers two and three," he murmured. "Law-abiding is rule number one."

Pinned in place by his look, the need to move grew unbearable. She crossed her legs and wiggled her dangling foot in agitation.

At five feet six, she'd never be considered outrageously tall. But he was six foot three, at the very least. And despite the easy tone and his almost-teasing words, there was nothing soft about him. He was all dark edginess, like a tightly coiled spring.

He's too much for you, Jax. Just keep your fat mouth shut.

But she knew she wouldn't. According to her friends, she lived with her heart on her sleeve. According to every foster family she'd ever been placed with, she simply lived with her foot in her smart-ass mouth. Realistically Jax knew the truth dwelled somewhere in between.

But the need to provoke him was too great.

Her leg stilled, and she adopted a wide-eyed, innocent air. "I still haven't addressed the most critical issue. The age-old question—boxers or briefs?"

"I wouldn't classify that as an age-old question," he said, and the corners of his eyes crinkled as he smiled, the first show of frank amusement.

Blinking hard, Jax stared at him. She'd thought it had been a fluke, but her first impression had been spot-on. He was *extra* hot when humored.

Fascinated, she continued. "Sure it is. Ranks right up there with the chicken-versus-egg question." She noticed a small scar that disappeared under a dark slash of eyebrow, daring to mar all that perfection. "And the argument over which is more influential, nature or nurture."

Intense interest flared in his face. "I wasn't aware men's underwear was as hotly contested as genes versus environment in forming personality."

"In certain circles it is," she said.

A droll skepticism crossed his face. "None that I frequent."

"That's not saying much. And as far as DNA and environment are concerned…" Jax's face softened with the faded memories of her grandmother belting out the latest country-western song. "I've always believed we're a unique combination of the two."

Pursing his lips, his voice turned thoughtful. "I've always hoped we could overcome them both."

Intriguing response. *Very* intriguing.

Troubled by the notion, she studied his scar, wondering about its origin. "Is that why you wear a suit? To overcome your DNA?"

The twinkle in his eyes grew brighter. "A better question would be, is psychoanalysis via underwear a required course as a music therapist?"

Amused, Jax swept a stray hair from her cheek. "No. But every choice you make reveals a little of your character. Today proves I lead with my heart." She studied his endless legs, encased in what had to be custom-fit trousers, giving a decisive nod before going on. "You're definitely a briefs man. You like everything neatly—" she lifted her gaze to his for effect "—*contained*."

A quick flash of a devilish grin morphed from outrageously handsome to downright devastating, and the euphoric high it produced only made her miss the smile more when it was gone. Disturbed by the thought, she sent him a pointed look, and her voice lost the teasing tone. "Including your emotions."

His scar shifted in surprise at her blunt statement, and she was almost ashamed she felt so smug about bringing the man down a notch.

Apparently, he didn't agree.

"I think I'll let the insinuation my emotions are contained in my underwear pass without comment," he finally said. His faint smile was concerning. "Especially since my deal with my sister includes further contact with you."

Confused, and more than a little alarmed, Jax frowned. "How does your deal with Nikki include further contact between us?"

"She didn't tell you the details?" His tone implied he wasn't at all surprised his sister had been less than forthcoming. "In exchange for helping you, she promised me she'd finally let me hire someone to move in with us and help her with her daily activities until she's out of her cast."

"And how does that affect *me*?"

He settled back and shot her a master-of-all-he-surveyed smile. "Because the live-in caretaker is going to be you."

CHAPTER TWO

BLAKE WATCHED JAX go completely still before the refusal burst from her lips.

"No." Clearly stunned, Jax froze for a few more seconds filled with silence before she continued, "Wait, let me put that another way," she said leaning closer, bringing the smell of lemon shampoo and damp earth. "*Hell*, no."

Fighting back a smile, Blake said, "That was eloquent."

"That was clearer."

"Why the emphatic refusal? Nikki told me the cut in funding has forced the club to shut down several programs, including yours. So obviously you're in need of a job."

"No, I'm in need of a plan to get the programs up and running again." A furrow appeared between her eyebrows. "And no offense, Suit," she said smoothly, but Blake got the sense she did mean to offend, "but I'm not in bad enough straits to accept a job that requires me to live in your home."

The words lingered in the air between them as Blake held her gaze. Awareness seeped into the limo and saturated every molecule of air, making each breath suddenly feel heavy. And then Jax turned to face forward, effectively putting an end to the moment.

Part of him echoed her reluctance. But so far Nikki had fired the three people he'd hired to help. And she'd refused the limo service he occasionally used. Blake had nearly burst a fuse when he'd discovered his sister had driven herself to the flash mob in a cast.

A *long leg* cast.

Which was as reckless as the careless stunt that had broken her leg in the first place. It was amazing she hadn't gotten herself killed today. And if he didn't get Nikki to accept help from somebody, she'd wind up dead in a car accident, just like his father.

For a flickering moment, the memories flooded him and his chest grew tight, making breathing difficult.

Blake rubbed his forehead, easing the tension as he concentrated on the view out the tinted window. Palm trees paraded past like guards along the median. Cars eased forward in sporadic burps as the city reached the peak of the Friday rush hour. His sister was going to drive him stark, raving mad. The past few years had been tough, the two of them clashing more and more. Now he suspected she was doing things solely with the intent to tick him off.

And how could he concentrate on the biggest case of his career if he was living on pins and needles, dreading her next stunt? He needed someone to help Nikki, and the only one she'd agreed on was the hellion on heels.

He glanced at said hellion. Unfortunately, his fleeting impression at the courthouse had been dead-on. Jax Lee was trouble of monumental proportions. Impulsive. Headstrong. With a mouth to match.

Worse…everything about her made him hot.

Honey-colored hair, wild and unrestrained, hung in waves down her back, while the small tattoo on the inside of her right wrist enhanced her unruly air. And, as if that weren't disturbing enough, her long legs were bare beneath the cutoffs. Her black cowboy boots were decorated with a line of red thread that twined around the ankles and climbed higher, as if wanting to hold more of her close; he knew the feeling.

Curbing his reaction had been doable until he'd discovered the sound body had indeed come with a sound mind, the sharp wit and keen intellect triggering a need the likes of which he could no longer ignore. Unfortunately, intellect did not equal common sense. Or sanity. Her amusing mouth was sassier than all his past girlfriends' combined, but her reckless nature made her a risk.

A risk he had no choice but to take.

Pushing the doubts aside, Blake settled back and focused on the oddly enticing sight of her lightly jiggling foot. Obviously, the lady was incapable of holding still.

Or keeping her opinions to herself.

"What will it take to change your mind?" he said. "Money?"

She rolled her eyes, as if to say his attempt was lame.

"Whatever your weekly salary is, I'll triple it," he said.

"No thanks," she said smoothly. "I'm sure you can find someone else."

"Nikki refuses a hired aid. And the only other family I have is my mother, but she was the one who encouraged Nikki to drive herself to the courthouse today." At Jax's curious look, he felt obligated to attempt to explain Abigail Bennington, an impossible feat. "My mother doesn't believe in setting limits."

A fact that had been okay when his father had still been alive. After his death, Blake had been the one left to pick up the slack, striving to see that a then twelve-year-old headstrong Nikki made it to adulthood in one piece. No easy task.

He tipped his head. "As a matter of fact, you and my mother would get along great. She believes everyone should lead with their heart, too."

The smile she sent was laced with a touch of reproach. "Smart lady."

"Yes. But my mother also believes in love potions, tarot cards and the validity of the psychic hotline," Blake said drily. "So take that for what it's worth."

Her smile grew bigger. "Your mother sounds wonderful."

Abigail Bennington was frustrating. Exasperating. And notoriously unreliable. As much as he cared about her, dealing with his mom wasn't always easy. Luckily, she was also very lovable in her own wacky way.

Wacky, just like the beautiful woman with the tiny tattoo. Her wrist rested on her lap, and he discreetly tried to make out the picture. But he only managed to get an eyeful of a bare, tanned and very toned thigh.

A few more moments passed filled with awareness, and he forced his eyes back to her face. "Look," he said reasonably, "Nikki needs company, and I'm currently involved in a case that's requiring a lot of my time. And my mother has a social calendar that would put the First Lady to shame." He blew out a breath. "Most of Nikki's old high school pals have moved away. And the few that still live here have jobs. Honestly," Blake went on thoughtfully, "I think she's missing her friends."

Jax's foot stopped its incessant wiggling, and she crossed her arms, a small frown stealing across her face as she nibbled on her lower lip. Obviously she was rethinking her refusal, more moved by compassion than money. Information he fully intended to take advantage of.

"Nikki had been looking forward to her summer break for months," he said, pressing on. He'd had years of practice reading juries, and Jax's sympathy was easy to see. He almost had her. "Now she's stuck at home. What she needs is someone closer to her age for company." Truthfully, he thought his sister needed a keeper, but he kept that tidbit to himself. "So she won't feel so...alone."

Jax heaved out a sigh, turning to face him. "Okay, I'll do it." Blake's blood surged in triumph. "But I have one condition," she said.

"Which is?"

"I want you to handle my legal problem."

The triumphant feeling collapsed. "I'm a federal prosecutor, not a defense attorney."

"I can't afford to hire a lawyer, even with the tripled salary."

Blake frowned. "So you'll be assigned a public defender. Most of them are excellent. And more than capable of handling your case."

"Sorry, Suit," she said, her gaze suddenly serious. "I entered the foster system when I was ten years old, which means I've dealt with a lot of social workers through the years. I learned to spot a bad one a mile away." The tidbit about her past was disturbing. But there was no self-pity in her eyes, just a level of acceptance that was impressive, and Blake fought the surge of sympathy. "Suffice it to say," she went on, "I've had enough experience with government employees to be a little leery of the devoted public servant. Yes, I might get lucky and be assigned an excellent attorney." She shot him a look that dared him to disagree. "But I also know how bad it will be if I'm appointed one that isn't."

Her hazel eyes exhibited a wariness and knowledge beyond her years, a hard-earned wisdom bubbling just beneath surface. Too bad she didn't apply that wisdom on a regular basis. Blake shifted in his seat, wishing he could offer her words of assurance. But he had more than enough experience to know that a poorly executed defense could have lifelong consequences.

And clearly Jacqueline Lee knew it, too.

"Consider it an exchange of favors," she said with a stubborn lift of her chin. And he supposed somewhere in that zany world she inhabited the logic made sense. "If you want me to help you with Nikki, those are my terms."

With his current schedule, their arrangement would mean burning the midnight oil. But he wouldn't be getting any work done if he was worried that Nikki would hobble to her car and drive across town again, just to obtain a second cast tattoo.

Blake wearily rubbed a hand down his face and then shot Jax a hard look. "You'll have to follow my directions to the letter."

"I can do that."

"Which means no arguing over my every instruction."

Her attempt to feign ignorance was comical. "I'm very capable of holding my tongue."

All evidence to date suggested otherwise.

He paused for effect and then raised a doubtful eyebrow. "I guess we'll find out," he murmured.

Her gaze didn't budge, and the challenge in her voice was another gut-clenching jolt to his libido. "I guess we will."

The next morning Jax left Nikki relaxing by her brother's sparkling pool, tablet computer in hand, and made her way up the bougainvillea-lined walk leading to the main house. Since Jax's quarters were located in a separate guest cottage beyond the pool, avoiding the owner so far had been easy. The rest of the day would likely be a different story.

For the bazillionth time since she'd said yes, Jax questioned her decision to accept the temporary job. In the end, it hadn't been because she needed the money desperately, which was true, or that the flexibility of the work would afford her time to pursue funding for the club, which was also accurate. Ultimately, the mention of Nikki's loneliness had won her over.

Jax had spent years living in homes surrounded by people, yet feeling all alone.

But for the first time, alone was sounding almost attractive. Putting up with Blake's disturbing presence in the limo had been bad enough, but now she was staying on his property. As his *employee*. And the thought of being reduced to a subordinate to the strictly by-the-book man was less than thrilling. Eight years spent at the mercy of the foster-care system had instilled in her an inherent dislike of being under an authoritative thumb. Either way, as frustrating as he was, she knew he was an excellent lawyer. *Brilliant* was the word Nikki had used. Which would have made the exchange of favors perfect…except for that damn coolly amused attitude of his yesterday.

An attitude that had only gotten worse.

Because last night, when the limo had arrived in front of the courthouse to drop her off, her car had been missing. After a brief moment of panic on her part, Blake had phoned the police station with her license plate…and learned her VW Beetle had been towed and impounded for a parking violation.

Which meant that the day that had started out good before turning bad had officially landed on the ugly.

She'd wound up having to endure Blake's patient yet imposing form in her apartment while she packed for his house—the light in his eyes clearly communicating he was even more amused since she'd added a parking violation to her list of crimes. It was stupid, she knew, to care that the man thought she was a complete flake.

Unfortunately, now she needed to remind him of that very fact by asking him for a ride to the impound lot to retrieve her car.

Jax bit back the groan as dread and an annoying sliver of anticipation wormed its way into her limbs, and she rubbed a damp palm down her jeans as she passed through the French doors and into the foyer. She paused, wondering where to look for Blake, feeling underdressed in her well-worn jeans.

His modern, U-shaped house was framed in wood and stone and gorgeously situated in an exclusive island neighborhood in South Miami Beach. Jax headed into the huge living room, where dark Brazilian wood floors added warmth. Massive floor-to-ceiling windows afforded an unobstructed view of the Biscayne Bay to the north, and to the south, the pool nestled between the U.

All in all, a soothing scene…until she spied Blake at the far end of the room.

Jax's heart picked up speed even as her stride grew slower as she considered leaving before being detected. After yesterday's trail of humiliating moments, she longed to rejoin Nikki at the pool and forget about her car. Unfortunately, the sound of her squeaking tennis shoes announced her arrival, and Blake turned before she could decide whether to pay now or pay later.

Her heart shifted from First to Third as he approached, long legs crossing the vast room with a purpose.

Clean-shaven and impeccably dressed, Blake looked almost as formal as the day before. The tux had been replaced with charcoal-colored pants and a white dress shirt, and his thick, ink-black hair was damp at the edges, probably from a shower.

Didn't he know it was Saturday? And why couldn't she convince her libido that he was so not her type that she couldn't even begin to count the ways? The oodles of dollars in his bank account didn't come close to making her list of concerns, but she was dying to know where his fortune came from.

"Please don't tell me you're accepting bribes from the Mafia," she said.

His pace slowed as he approached, puzzlement briefly hijacking his cool demeanor. "I'm sorry?"

Not near as sorry as she was when he stopped in front of her and she was hit with his now familiar cologne. Tamping down the wave of heat, she shifted her gaze from his broad shoulders, emphasized by the cut of his shirt, to his striking face.

Her body might never get used to the masculine beauty.

"No matter how far up the chain he is, there is no way a government attorney could afford a house like this," she said with a wry hike of her brow. "Unless, of course, he's on the take."

His cool expression morphed to one of interest, and the gray eyes crinkled at the edges in humor. "I promise, I'm not accepting bribes. And trust me," he said, his voice achieving the perfect droll note, "no one enters a life of public law for the salary. I'm fortunate enough that the paycheck isn't a concern." He held her gaze a moment before turning his attention to the view, his face briefly growing hard. "I inherited my money."

Inherited. Which meant someone—*family*—had to die for him to acquire all this wealth. And judging by the look on his face it was a subject she should stay far, far away from. Because something in his expression told her if she pursued that line of questioning, he'd cut her off at the knees.

A perplexing and exasperating tenderness welled inside her. The man who had the world at his feet had a vulnerable spot, too. And, minus the inheritance part, one she could relate to, no less.

Toes tapping nervously, she struggled to lighten the mood again before she asked for a ride, ignoring her clamoring nerves. "Well, I guess I have to change my first impression of you as the James Bond type." He quirked his eyebrow skeptically, and she went on. "Must have been the tux."

His forehead bunched in amusement. "Must have been."

"But the ultrarich guy fighting for justice is more Batman than James Bond," she said, struggling to mirror his coolly amused demeanor.

A quick flash of a sexy half grin graced his face, and Jax's breath caught, her world tipping sideways.

"Except Batman was a vigilante operating outside of the law." Clearly playing along, he crossed his arms, his dress shirt stretching across broad shoulders. "And for the record, I prefer the tux to tights."

The planted image did nothing to right her still-spinning world as she pictured his muscular legs encased in formfitting fabric. And the thought of a man in tights should *not* be turning her on.

"Interesting visual," she murmured, her tone holding an embarrassingly husky quality.

Their eyes locked.

Time stretched.

And Jax struggled to shore up her body's defenses against the attraction she'd just let slip. She could tell by the wary look in Blake's eyes.

Big mistake, Jax. Big mistake.

Right now climbing into a car and riding across town with the man hardly seemed like a good idea. But without her vehicle, she was stuck in his house with no means of escape, even for a brief reprieve.

She swallowed hard and bit the proverbial bullet. "I was hoping you could give me a ride to the impound parking lot."

He pressed his lips together, either biting back a smile or suppressing a groan of irritation. Jax wasn't sure which would be worse.

"I'm free this afternoon," he said, and she sighed, relieved that the car ride would be delayed. "I have some work to finish this morning. But first we need to discuss the terms of our employment agreement," he added.

Her heart slipped to her belly.

Damn. And escape had been so near at hand.

When he headed toward the door, she sighed and followed him into the hallway, praying his office was as big as the living room. Because, as she'd learned in the limo, being confined in a small space with the lethally sexy Blake Bennington was an assault on her senses she was ill-equipped to deal with. All she wanted was to survive the contract negotiations without adding to her growing list of embarrassing moments.

But given her interactions with the exasperating hottie to date, she wasn't holding out much hope.

Blake leaned back in his leather chair, elbows on the armrests, fingers steepled just beneath his chin. Fortunately, his monstrous desk separated him from Jax as she paced back and forth, reading through the contracts.

Sporting threadbare jeans and a Madonna T-shirt—did the woman own anything that didn't have a face plastered on it?—she looked fresh and surprisingly at ease in his office of hunter-green and dark leather furniture. Her unruly hair had been whipped into submission, a long braid extending down her back, streaks of gold intertwined with the honey tones. At first glance he'd thought the restrained hairstyle would help control his growing appreciation for her looks.

But he'd been wrong. Because the graceful neck along with her loose-limbed, lissome body conjured images of her dance routine gone awry. And the reminder of her hips swinging to the Latino hip-hop song was hardly conducive to controlling his appreciation. Not to mention the husky voice radiating from the capricious female earlier in the living room. The voice that had broadcast that she wanted him, too...

A slow burn took up residence in his gut, heating him from the inside out. Ignoring his own desire was a lot harder now that he was certain it was returned.

Jax finished reading and halted beside his desk, her clear skin kissed by the sun and radiating health. Hazel eyes assessed him doubtfully as she set the contracts in front of him.

"Is this really necessary?" she said.

"It's a fairly standard employment contract."

She leaned her hands on his desk, which had the unfortunate effect of placing her breasts closer to eye level. "Seems like an awful lot of words just to say I'm hired, explain a few rules and list my hourly rate," she said doubtfully.

Studiously ignoring the view, Blake reached for the document. "No one should enter into employment without laying out the terms of their agreement."

Maintaining his businesslike demeanor was difficult enough after spending ten minutes admiring her features.

And he wasn't above admitting a few fantasies had been entertained by the sight.

He cleared his throat, hoping to put an end to the torture by getting her to sign...and leave him in peace. "This protects your interests as well by covering the terms of the dissolution of your employment should the relationship not work out."

Blake mentally flinched at the term *relationship*. But Jax didn't seem to notice. She was too busy looking at him as if he'd just crawled out of an alien spacecraft.

She straightened up and crossed her arms, which obscured Madonna's face and pushed Jax's breasts higher. He shifted slightly in his seat, willing his groin *not* to respond.

"Do you ever get tired of being this careful?" she said with amazement. "I mean—wow." Sweeping a stray lock of hair from her cheek, she eyed him closely. "I've never met anyone so cautious. Your muscles must be tired from all the overtime they put in being—" she clenched both her fists to emphasize her point "—tensed and poised for every possible catastrophe." Hands relaxing, she dropped them to her sides, her hazel eyes boldly honest, her tone dry. "'Cuz this is only my second day of knowing you, and you're already exhausting me."

Trying to hide the grin, Blake wiped his hand across his chin and lower lip. She looked younger than her years, fresh and beautiful—with a youthful exuberance that was captivating. Exhaustion hardly seemed to be her problem. His libido, on the other hand...?

That was getting a vigorous workout.

Wishing she'd at least sit down so there was less of her to see and admire, he reached for the papers. "I'm not 'tensed for every catastrophe,' as you put it. I'm just being practical. Preparing an exit strategy ahead of time makes life easier for everyone," he said smoothly.

"Don't you ever just loosen up and let life happen?"

"No." He slid the document forward, hoping she'd take the

hint and finish the task at hand. "Because I might not like what life hands me."

A barking scoff escaped from her mouth. "Since when did planning in advance guarantee to prevent tragedy?"

The innocently spoken statement knocked him hard, bringing the memories along, and he froze. The biggest tragedy in his life—his father's death—had been precipitated by Blake's carelessness...at a time when he'd been so sure he hadn't a care in the world.

He'd been a thoughtless college frat kid that never gave a damn about the consequences of his actions.

His chest cinched tight and he locked the memories away, trying to subdue a frown. "I didn't say planning guaranteed a tragedy-free life." He lifted a brow meaningfully at the disturbingly beautiful woman standing before him. "But flying by the seat of your pants doesn't help, either."

They stared at each other a moment more, and he inched the document closer to her, using his best let's-finish-this-up tone. "Do you want to have a lawyer review this for you?"

She shot him a look that suggested he was insane, and he realized he'd be hard-pressed to offer up a defense. "As of right now," she said, "you're the only lawyer I know."

Tipping his head, he steadily held her gaze. "Unfortunately, my advice would be useless." He gestured toward the agreements. "Conflict of interest and all."

Jax parked a hip on the top of his desk. A flash of tanned, toned thigh peeked through the frayed hole in her jeans, briefly tripping up his train of thought and setting off a wail of warning in his head.

"I have an overwhelming urge to ask you to do just that," she said as she looked down at him. "Something tells me if the contract wasn't in my best interests..." her pursed lips twisted into a grin "...you'd rat yourself out." Her grin grew bigger, hazel eyes sparkling with amusement. "I'd love to see that."

Blake's internal siren grew louder. Her position, as well

as the knowledge the attraction was mutual, made her all the more alluring.

"I can assure you, the contract is designed to protect us both," he said as he leaned back in his seat, seeking distance.

She loosely shrugged her shoulders. "I believe you."

"You should show a little more caution in the future." His eyebrows crept higher. "Next time you might be dealing with someone who isn't so trustworthy."

"You exude trustworthiness. And at the risk of sounding like a lawyer basher, I doubt you learned that skill in law school. Are you a former Eagle Scout?"

"No."

"Boy Scout?"

"No."

"Come on, fess up." Perched on the desk above him, she leaned closer, as if to share a secret, and shot him a teasing smile. Her sweetly spiced scent filled his nose, eliciting sensual visions, and his heart began to work harder at her proximity, even as he fought to maintain a calm expression. "In your youth you helped little old ladies cross the street, right?" she said.

Hardly. He'd spent his younger years with a rebellious streak a mile wide. And he'd fought long and hard to subdue the genetic tendencies his sister and mother wielded without a care. But his carefree days were long gone.

Blake calmly asked, "Are you going to sign the agreement or not?"

Delicately arched eyebrows pinched together in amusement. "I'm just here to help Nikki with her daily activities and drive her around. What could possibly go wrong?"

Lips twisting wryly at her words, his mind filled with the possibilities. But it was only one that consumed his mind. He could slip up, get lost in the sexual fog that enveloped him every time she was near.

His voice grew rough at the thought. "A great many things could go wrong."

The worst of which would involve touching this woman.

As she held his gaze, the amused glint in her eyes slowly faded, replaced by something else, and tension billowed thick around them. He had the distinct impression she was finally considering just how...wrong, for lack of a better word, this living arrangement could become.

Or perhaps his traitorous libido had finally made itself known to the woman.

Frowning, she nibbled at a corner of her mouth, and Blake's eyes were drawn to the process before moving on to her partially parted lips. Pink, soft and infinitely kissable lips. Which ultimately proved his downfall.

Because when her amused smile returned, he knew she'd caught him staring.

Fantasizing.

Her tone of voice and her words gave her away. "Would you feel more at ease if we inserted a no-kissing clause?"

Instantly, desire flared. Incinerating his thoughts. And every cell in his body demanded he pull her head down and take that too-sassy mouth with his. The seconds passed agonizingly slow, blood surging as the internal battle raged.

Lust versus reason.

Need versus duty.

Selfish college frat kid versus responsible adult.

Sweat prickled along his hairline as Blake mentally built a case against the insane craving to pull her onto his lap and give in to the fierce urge. Most notably, he needed a woman who fit with his life. One who was predictable. Rational. Jax was clearly neither of these. So why was he still contemplating kissing her?

Annoyed at himself, he removed a pen from the brass container on his desk, holding it out to Jax. "That won't be necessary. Let's just make sure everything goes smoothly."

After a moment's consideration, she took the pen and dropped her attention to the contract, scrawling her signature along the bottom with a carelessness that matched the woman herself. For a moment, he was distracted by the glimpse of the lacy pink bra beneath her shirt. The gentle cleavage. A view that was cut off when she pushed off his desk and stood, tossing the pen next to the contract.

"If that's all," she said, "I'm rejoining Nikki at the pool."

Relieved, he gave a curt nod. "I'll find you when I'm ready to drive you to your car."

His gazed lingered on the agile swing of her long legs and the gentle sway of her hips as she exited, and he tightened his grip on his pen...doubting the sanity of hiring Jax. Which was confirmed when he caught a glimpse of their employment contract, where, right after he'd listed the job description and duties, Jax had added a single line: *No kissing allowed.*

With a groan, he leaned back in his chair, trying to decide if he should feel relieved he'd just solved his Nikki problem. Or alarmed he'd created an even bigger one with Jax.

CHAPTER THREE

EYES FIXED ON the middle-aged man inside the small, glassed-in booth of the run-down parking lot, Jax carefully kept the panic from her tone as she leaned closer to the speaker in the window, acutely aware of Blake's gaze on her.

"What do you mean I can't retrieve my car until Monday? We still live in a democracy, don't we? I have a right to retrieve my property, don't I?" she said to the attendant, pointing at her old VW Beetle parked among all the other cars surrounded by a chain-link fence.

Jailed, just as she had been. And it wasn't fair her car should pay the penalty for her mistakes.

"Cry me a river, lady." Perched on his stool, the man swiped a hand through his thinning hair in irritation. "Next time don't park your car in a two-hour parking spot and leave it there for six hours."

"I got arrested," she said, her face flooding with heat at her poorly worded defense. But there was no taking back the overshare now. "I couldn't move my car."

"It's not my fault you got tossed in the slammer," he said, and Jax forced her chin higher. "And I ain't the one making the rules, either," he went on. "I'm just paid to follow them."

"What rule dictates that I have to go to the city municipal building first?"

"The one that applies to a previous unpaid parking ticket

of yours. And the order states you can't get your car until you pay that delinquent fine. And you can't pay that fine until Monday morning at nine o'clock."

Jax opened her mouth to protest, but Blake interrupted.

"Then Monday morning it is. Thanks for your help," Blake said smoothly, taking her elbow.

His touch brought back the memory of being in his office, the overwhelming need to kiss him, and every muscle in Jax's body tensed. Despite his cool demeanor, she knew he was dying to make a comment about her delinquent parking ticket. The one she'd stuffed into the bottom of her purse. And with all the turmoil at the club recently, it hadn't been high on her priorities.

Just one more sin stacked up on her towering pile of crimes.

And her need to secure a bit of freedom from Blake was escalating by the minute. The purposefully bland expression. The glimmer of amusement in his eyes. Not to mention her growing obsession with those broad shoulders, the lean hips and those lips…

As he led her back to his car, she hoped she didn't sound as desperate as she felt. "I need my vehicle."

"You can use Nikki's until Monday," he said reasonably.

A frown threatened. "But right now we're not far from South Glade Teen Center. I was planning on leaving here and swinging by to check in with everybody."

"I'll take you."

Her heart tanked. Great. More time cooped up with Blake in his car. The ride over had been strained as they'd both diligently ignored her additional condition on the contract, an impulsive decision on her part. But she hadn't been able to stop herself, because Blake had been looking at her as if he wanted to kiss her and was dismayed by the thought at the same time. Not exactly an ego booster. And the last time a man had looked at her like that—with the combination of desire and a doubting-her-sanity look—she'd vowed she wouldn't put herself into that position again....

Her stomach knotted as she remembered the expression on Jack's face—the man she'd once hoped to build a permanent relationship with. Maybe even, God forbid, start a *family*.

Because who didn't want a core group of people, or at least one other person, to whom you always belonged? Someone to lean on when the world turned cruel and unusual. Outside of the teen center, the concept of a permanent home had eluded her since she was ten years old. As a grown-up she'd finally been free to create one of her own. After a false start—her former boyfriend a massive disappointment, to say the least—she'd finally realized she didn't need a man to achieve her goal.

The club had been all the family she needed.

She looked longingly at her beautiful, beat-up Beetle and let out a sigh. And she'd been so looking forward to escaping Blake's presence in exchange for a visit to the center—her safe place since her adolescent days—giving her nervous system a much-needed holiday.

As they neared his sleek Lexus, Blake said, "I'm curious. Why do you need to go by the club?" He rounded to the driver's side, looking at her over the hood. "To check in with the kids you're supposed to be providing a good example to?"

She shot him a lethal look as she opened the passenger side and then dropped into the seat, pulling the door closed with a hard thunk.

Blake slipped into the driver's seat. "And do tell," he went on, closing his door and turning to face her, clearly struggling to maintain an impassive expression, "what other life lessons do you teach besides getting arrested, parking illegally and not paying your traffic fines?"

She refused to grind her teeth in annoyance. And it would be so much easier if he'd just go ahead and laugh at her with those sensual lips, so he could move on to more important things.

Like kissing her.

The sexual tension, the awareness, was a living, fire-breathing thing that was so much worse when enclosed in small spaces with the infuriating man. Especially now that she knew it was mutual.

Damn it.

"Trespassing?" Thickly fringed eyes on her, he went on lightly, listing the possibilities. "Shoplifting?" The knot of attraction and irritation in her gut twisted harder as he went on. "Or maybe—"

Desperate to end the sarcasm, she placed her fingers on that maddening, sensual mouth, halting his words. And everything went still.

Except for the need surging through her body...

Blood whooshed in her ears as his gray eyes, flecked with gold, remained fixed on hers. Her nerve endings vibrated from the sensation of firm lips, smooth, stubble-free skin and warm breath seeping between her fingers. There was no mistaking the heat in his gaze or the tension in his body, clearly a combination of lust and steel—the steel communicating just how much he was humoring her by not calling her out on her impertinent move. And what would he be like if the lust won and he released all that careful control?

As she held his mouth, the seconds ticked by with only the faint sound of their breathing, until she finally controlled her own emotions enough to keep herself from doing something rash.

Either throttling him or tasting that sexy mouth, she wasn't sure which.

Her voice low, she forced herself to continue to meet his heated gaze. "You get one more comment, Suit. And then I'm cutting you off." Two heartbeats passed, long enough for her to wonder if he was again contemplating kissing her, and then she said, "Well?" She dropped her hand and raised a prompting eyebrow, braced for his last verbal jab. Would it be angry? Amused? Or, God help her, sexual? "What's the comment going to be?"

The pause was brief, but the intensity in his eyes scorched her insides, leaving the moment feeling longer than it was. "I think that with your lifestyle," he said, his voice huskily amused, as if struggling between the dueling notions of humor and sex, "you should keep a full-time lawyer on retainer."

Irritated by his words, Jax pressed her lips together and pivoted to face forward, crossing her arms to contain her thrumming heart in her chest. "Just turn on the car and drive."

Blake parked on the street in front of the South Glade Teen Center and turned off his car, looking doubtfully at the old downtown warehouse that had been converted into a club for kids. Alarm bells were ringing in his head again, the same ones that had sounded earlier when Jax had touched him. But this alert was of a nonsexual kind and triggered by his environment.

To say that the club was located in a questionable part of town was being generous.

"It doesn't look safe to park here," he said.

"It isn't," Jax said with a careless tone as they exited the Lexus and headed for the front door. "But with your fancy security system, I doubt anyone will steal your car. Of course, that won't keep some random kids from having fun."

The alarm crept higher. "Fun?"

"You know, doing a little redecorating with spray paint or a set of keys," she said. Frowning, he opened the door to let her into the building, and she shot him a saccharine-sweet grin as she passed by. "Maybe a tire iron or two."

Her tone was unconcerned. But then again, it wasn't her car. Or maybe the many dents in her old Beetle were from a tire iron, as well.

His lips twisted wryly. "Thanks for the warning," he said, following her inside.

They headed deeper into the building, passing clusters of kids of various ages and ethnicities. Although they eyed Blake with suspicion, each group was clearly excited to see Jax, some of the preteens rushing to give her a hug. The older ones were too cool for outward displays of affection, but beneath their ribbing and sarcastic comments lay a fondness that was impossible to miss.

And with each acknowledgment, Jax grew more relaxed, her previous tension evaporating as she ruffled heads and dispensed smiles, heading for the stairwell on the far side of the gym. They passed a contentious game of basketball involving a dozen lanky male adolescents, and several called out in greeting to Jax, joking about her arrest. She waved in reply and returned each verbal jab with a quip of her own, obviously knowing each kid's history, leaving the players laughing as she started up the narrow stairway to the second floor.

"I'll just swing by the office and check my mail," she said to Blake. "I also need to get my guitar from my locker."

"A guitar?" He wasn't particularly surprised by her choice of instrument, and he tried hard to ignore the delicious curve of her backside, the seductive sway of hips just several steps in front of him as their footsteps echoed in the small, shabby stairwell. "Do you take requests?"

She kept her back to him. "I doubt I know anything you'd like to hear."

"How about Lynyrd Skynyrd's 'Free Bird'?"

Surprise brought her head around with a jerk. "'Free Bird'?" Her eyebrows lowered in doubt, and her footsteps slowed. "I never would have pegged you for an old Southern rock fan."

"I'm not," he said, suppressed humor bunching his brow. "But anyone who's been bailed out of jail should have 'Free Bird' as their theme song."

Her eyes slowly narrowed as she stopped and faced him, raising his heart rate. Her location on the stairs brought them eye to eye, her mouth level with his.

The perfect position for capturing those lips.

"Your ability to deliver a subtle slap on the wrist is extraordinary, Suit," she said silkily. "It takes real talent to chastise someone in the same breath as a musical request." Her smile didn't quite reach her eyes, but the awareness did. "But I have my own ideas for a personal theme song."

Voice huskier than usual, he said, "So what song would be most appropriate?"

She looked at him thoughtfully for a moment, as a small, purely female smile crept up her face. "Let's see." Mouth pursed, she pretended to give the question careful consideration, and he couldn't get past the image of her puckered lips. "I was thrown in jail for defending an institution that I believe in," she said, sending him a pointed look. "And then promptly chastised for my reckless behavior by a man who thinks he's living life on the edge when he ignores the do-not-remove-by-penalty-of-law tag on his mattress."

He barely managed to repress the image of her on his mattress. "I would never do that."

"Of course not. How about make a right on red when it's posted not to?"

"It's against the law," he said lightly.

Her hazel eyes flickered with heat. "Briefly park your car in the drop-off lane at the airport?"

"Illegal." He struggled to keep the sizzle from his gaze. "Not to mention inconsiderate."

Jax bit her delectable lip, clearly suppressing the grin as she turned and continued up, reaching the second floor and moving down an empty hallway. "So my willingness to risk an arrest for my cause is being questioned by a man who thinks I'm reckless for leaving home without an umbrella when there's a ten percent chance of rain. I'm thinking the most appropriate song for me is 'It's My Life' by Bon Jovi." She entered a small, cramped office with two desks and stopped, turning to face him again. "But that's only because I'm not aware of any songs entitled—" Jax leaned in, bringing her arousing, obstinate gaze closer "—'My Choices Are None of Your Damn Business.'"

She was near enough for him to see the flecks of brown and green in her eyes. But he didn't require a close-up view to see the fire snapping in her gaze, the stubborn insistence that she would do what she wanted and damn the consequences.

Including touching him…

The memory resurfaced, resurrecting the acute need she'd created when she'd held his lips. Her soft fingers. The heated skin. And the smell of vanilla filling the car. Suddenly he was struck with the realization that Jax's scent was always changing, as unpredictable as the woman herself.

With his heart pounding, his tone was rough as he dished up a dose of harsh reality. "Your choices are my business now."

At the reminder of her current living arrangements—made more alarming by the chemistry sizzling between them—time stretched. Expanded to impossible lengths. Gazes locked, the moment lasted ten forevers as awareness pulsed between them. Until they were interrupted by a woman about Jax's age as she poked her head through the doorway.

"Janet Bennet stopped by looking for you, Jax," the blonde said. Blake cleared his throat, willing his libido to heel, and Jax took a small step back as her coworker sent her an encouraging smile. "There's a private-practice therapy group in town that's looking to hire a music therapist, and she recommended you. Apparently the job is yours if you want it," the woman continued. "They can afford to pay you a lot better, too."

Looking unconcerned, Jax retrieved her mail from the cubbyholes lining one wall and began flipping through the envelopes. "I'll hold out until South Glade is back on its feet."

"You haven't heard?" her coworker said.

Eyes now alert, Jax looked up from her mail. "Heard what?"

"The board held an emergency meeting. Even if we get the funds back—"

"When," Jax said. Mail clutched tightly in her hand, she lowered her arms a bit. "Not if."

The blonde's face softened in sympathy. *"When* we get the funds, their rehiring of you depends on the outcome of your charges."

Jax's face lost a little of its color and a lot of its usual vitality, and an unwanted stab of sympathy hit Blake. Unable to stop himself, he stepped closer, placing a reassuring hand on her arm.

"Tell Janet I said thanks for thinking of me," Jax said, her voice strained. She sent Blake a look that was hard to interpret. "But I'll beat the charges."

And, without a word of warning, Jax headed out of the office, murmuring a thanks to her coworker as she passed. Blake sent the woman a polite smile and muttered an "excuse me" before following Jax out of the office. He caught up with her silent form as she neared a line of lockers along the scuffed hallway. The graceful sway of her hips was marked by a slight stiffness he knew was due to tension, and this time was not of the sexual kind.

Making her way down the line of lockers, she stopped at one and worked the lock. Her fingers took several tries to finagle the combination, and Blake's sympathy soared higher.

"You should take the job offer," he said.

She jerked the door open, the inside plastered with posters of bands and music artists, a wide assortment of country, rock, hip-hop and blues, just to name a few. Her jaw was set. "I'll wait until the club gets the money to reinstate the music program here."

He leaned a shoulder against the wall of lockers adorned with graffiti and crossed his arms as she pulled out her guitar.

"And what if they don't get the money?" he said.

"We will." Hand on the locker door, she turned to face him. "Because I'm going to make sure that we do."

"Okay," he said doubtfully, a part of him impressed by her perseverance—a by-product of her stubbornness, clearly— and her natural confidence.

But one thing he'd learned long ago: you couldn't change the world through sheer force of will. And he felt obligated to be the voice of reason. Because someone needed to be pragmatic and, just like with his own family, apparently that someone had to be him.

"What happens if the board doesn't approve of the outcome of your charges?" he said.

She closed the locker door firmly, the noise echoing down the empty hallway.

Her hazel eyes were steady on his, and her words left him uneasy. "I have an excellent lawyer, so I'm not concerned."

The next afternoon, teak oil and supplies in hand, Blake headed through the shelf-lined utility room of his home, looking forward to a few moments of peace and relaxation as he applied the oil to the railing on his boat. Tinkering with his catamaran was the perfect antidote to stress. He always started his Sundays—the only day he took off—by unwinding with the mindless activity. But today he'd spent the morning working on Jax's case.

And any time spent thinking about Jax was always disturbing.

For the hundredth time that day, his mind drifted back to yesterday and the feel of her fingers on his mouth. Unfortunately, even sleep hadn't provided him with an escape. Because last night he'd been tortured by dreams. Erotic, scorching dreams that would make facing her and keeping his thoughts to himself much more difficult. Desperate to free his mind of the perplexing woman, if only for a moment, Blake headed out the door and onto the pool deck…and then came to an abrupt halt.

His usually peacefully quiet pool was now inhabited by five females—his mother, Nikki and Jax, along with two adolescents he'd never met. Blake let out a frustrated groan.

He missed the days when retreat was possible.

He missed the days when Nikki was at college, worrying him from afar instead of from under his nose.

And he missed the days when his self-control wasn't subjected to repeated blows, the sight of Jax in shorts and a tank top, guitar in hand, revving up his heart in a manner that couldn't be good for his blood pressure.

Nikki and his mother sat in two chaise longues next to the poolside waterfall. Jax and the two unknown teens were engaged in what appeared to be a guitar lesson at the patio table, an open bag of caramels and candy wrappers scattered on top. The two adolescents were wearing baggy cargo pants, T-shirts and piercings that looked painful. On the basis of their age, he suspected they were attendees of her club.

"Blake!" his mother called, her salt-and-pepper hair sporting a pixie cut that flattered her lined face. "It's Sunday. Put that stuff down and do something that involves relaxation, for once."

His sister didn't give him a chance to respond.

"He can't, Mom. He's incapable of relaxation." Nikki, her black hair pulled into a ponytail, her gray eyes with a loaded look aimed in his direction, added an overly sweet smile to her barbs. "You know, most men spend their Sundays playing golf or watching football with a beer and a bucket of chicken wings."

Inwardly he braced for the conflict. Keeping his cool as Nikki needled him required Herculean effort.

"And most first-year law students spend their summers interning at a firm to gain work experience," he said drily. "Not encased in plaster from hip to toe from a zip-line accident."

A silly prank that had almost gotten her killed. Receiving the call from the E.R. about Nikki's accident had shaved several years off his life. He'd lived in dread of such a day, but had always suspected it would be due to a car accident. Nikki had spent her childhood champing at the bit, trying to grow up too fast. Now she drove too fast.

She *lived* too fast.

Leaving work and heading upstate to the hospital had put a massive strain on his workweek. But nothing compared to the gut-clenching memory of his little sister, pale and laid up in a hospital room with a concussion and a complicated fracture. And the fear of losing her, combined with the horrific memories of his father's accident, had scared him senseless. According to the doctor, she was lucky she hadn't been killed.

And it was good to know her mouth hadn't been injured in the process, either.

Nikki addressed their mother. "I told you he'd sneak in another jab about my mishap." She turned her attention back to Blake, narrowing her eyes. "You're still angry about the Times Square incident, aren't you?"

"No," he said. "I've moved on from your participation in a prank that involved a near brush with the police." Another incident that had required his efforts to smooth out—an incident that had been, as usual, dismissed as a kids-will-be-kids moment by his mother. "The next time you might actually get charged with something, which wouldn't bode well for your future as a lawyer, by the way," he finished drily.

The frown on his sister's face was small, but heartfelt. "Maybe you worry too much."

Blake remembered saying exactly those words to his father, and his gut churned.

Their gazes locked, and he went on in a low voice. "Maybe you don't worry enough."

After several tense seconds, filled with the sound of the waterfall and five pairs of female eyes on him, his mother reached over and patted Nikki on the hand.

"Take it easy on your brother, Nikki," his mother said lightly. "I suspect he just hasn't gotten any lately."

Three pairs of lids stretched wide at the remark, and he ignored the small, barking cough of surprise from Jax. The Bennington siblings didn't bat an eye. His mother didn't believe in a comment being too inappropriate to share. And while he was used to her casual attitude toward...hell, toward *everything*, it hardly set a good example for the youth among them.

"Why don't you ask that pretty lawyer out? You know, the one you were talking to at the courthouse?" Nikki said, surprising him with her words. When had Nikki seen Sara? "You two could have the perfect marriage, wear perfect matching suits and have two-point-five children together." She lifted an eyebrow wryly. "The perfect number, of course.

Blake was intensely aware of Jax's observant gaze, taking in the family interactions. Nikki and his mother had always been a dangerous combination, just as his father had warned. The two of them with Jax by their side might just do in Blake completely. And the fact that the merry band of estrogen appeared to be training new teenage recruits was alarming.

Taking on his family with an interested audience wasn't prudent. And Blake was intelligent enough to know when to cut his losses.

"Mom," he said evenly, "I'd appreciate it if you would refrain from making my social life a public discussion. And, Nikki..." He turned his attention to his sister. "I have enough on my hands with the family I've got."

And after a last glance at Jax, he turned and headed for the dock, grateful his boat, at least, was devoid of difficult women. But the question was, how long would the female-free moment last?

CHAPTER FOUR

WHEN NIKKI AND HER MOTHER had decided to retreat to the kitchen, Jax declined to go, claiming she wanted to relax in the sunshine. She was grateful Dawn and Tracy had accepted their invitation, because with everyone inside, Jax could study Blake, uninterrupted, as he moved about his luxury catamaran parked at the end the dock. The boat contained a glassed-in cabin and a cockpit lined with teak wood and royal-blue cushions. The crisp white sails provided a sharp contrast against the bright blue sky, sunlight dappling the palm-tree-lined, tropical waters of Biscayne Bay.

But the view paled in comparison to her first glimpse of Blake's mouthwatering physique in bathing trunks and a T-shirt. As far as Jax was concerned, a sharp legal mind should not be paired with a finely cut athlete's body. Either brains or brawn. It wasn't fair he had both. Perfect, just like his sister had teased.

Well, all except for the attitude.

His wide shoulders looked even broader stretched beneath a red T-shirt, and the black swim trunks revealed thighs to die for, his well-muscled legs obviously engaged in an ongoing love affair with the treadmill in his home gym. He'd covered the distance to the dock in record time, his retreat most likely fueled by a need to escape the family harassment by the pool. Or maybe he figured she might do something stupid again.

Like touching him.

Jax bit her lip and contemplated the enigmatic man that held her future in his hands, realizing she hadn't thanked him for his help yesterday. The setback with her car and the news of the board's decision had been unwelcome distractions. But she needed to rectify the oversight. She refused to feel ashamed of her arrest, but bad manners were absolutely unacceptable.

With a sigh and, unfortunately, something close to eager anticipation, she pushed up from her chair and padded barefoot across the pool deck and onto the warm wood of the dock.

And this time, Jax, keep your stupid, impulsive hands to yourself.

As she strode closer to the boat, Blake continued to swipe the paintbrush along the rail with long, even strokes.

Without looking up, he said, "I see you met my mother."

"Yes," she said. The scent of teak wood mixed with the salty breeze as water lapped gently against the boat. All of which should have been relaxing, and would have been but for the inconveniently disturbing view of Blake's hard body. "She was instructing me on how to prepare the perfect mojito," she said as she sent him a smile from the dock. "Apparently she grows her own ingredients."

"She planted lime trees and mint in her yard," he said. "She calls it her liquor garden."

The faint quirk to his lips was a mixture of amusement and warmth, with a trace of resigned exasperation, and Jax's grin grew bigger. As unconventional as his mother was, it was clear their relationship was one of affection and acceptance.

She stepped up onto the boat, admiring the forty-foot catamaran. Shading her eyes from the sun, she studied him as he went through the motions of dipping his paintbrush into the shallow pan and meticulously stroking the brush along the rail lining the deck. His focus and attention to detail weren't a surprise, and she imagined he'd make love the same way, the thought throwing her heart into a frenzy.

No touching, Jax. No touching!

But she refused to pretend she hadn't given the matter a great deal of thought already. His past actions led her to believe he'd take his time and linger, enjoying every sensation along the way. But then again, sometimes, like after she'd leaned close while perched on his desk, and *especially* when she'd touched his lips in his car yesterday...

Her heart thumped in her chest.

During *those* times, his eyes told her a different story, suggesting that one right move on her part and he would explode in a burst of flames that would incinerate them both.

A surge of longing started in the pit of her stomach and seeped outward, fueling the already rapid pace of her pulse. And she couldn't shake the question, was there a fiercely passionate man lurking beneath that coolly authoritative, frustratingly methodical exterior?

Blake interrupted her thoughts. "I assume you were giving those two girls guitar lessons."

She inhaled deeply, clearing her wayward thoughts. "Yes. And when I had breakfast with Nikki this morning, she said you wouldn't mind if they came to my guest cottage." She lightly nibbled on her cheek. Now that she'd seen the siblings in action, she wasn't so confident of his sister's assessment. "I hope that's true."

"As far as I'm concerned, my home is your home for as long as you're here." He shot her a look she couldn't interpret, but was loaded with warnings and meaning. "Within reason, of course."

There was a pause, his gray gaze fixed on hers, and the moment shifted to one filled with an awareness that was growing day by day. But in an effort to stick to her hands-off rule, she chose to ignore the undertones.

"Who chose the time and location of your flash mob?" he said.

Jax bunched her brow in surprise at the abrupt change in topic. "We all were bandying about ideas, but ultimately we went with Nikki's suggestion."

At her words, the truth suddenly became obvious, and Jax closed her eyes. *Nikki.* Of course. Why hadn't the idea occurred to her before?

Lifting her lids, she met his gaze. "You think she placed us there that day on purpose."

"Absolutely," he said. "Nikki overheard my phone call with Sara earlier in the week."

"Sara?" she said, remembering the gorgeous woman in the gorgeous suit. "You mean the lady you're supposed to somehow have half of a perfect child with?"

His eyes crinkled in humor. "That's the one. She agreed to meet with me at the courthouse Friday to give me some information in reference to a case I'm working on," he said, and then his brow bunched in aggravation. "And when my sister spied us coming down the steps, she turned on the music, effectively starting the event."

Jax pondered this for a moment and then tipped her head curiously. "Why would she go to such lengths to ensure you were there to see our flash mob?"

The tension around his eyes was impossible to miss. "To rub her participation in my face," he said. "To get back at me."

"And what did you do to warrant the payback?"

At her direct insult, he went completely still, and Jax wished she could take her words back. Not that she didn't mean them. However, insulting her current employer probably wasn't the best way to proceed. But living with her foot in her smart-ass mouth had almost become a way of life.

The lines of humor around his eyes returned. "Why are you so sure I deserve a payback?"

Since her mouth would only get her into more trouble,

she elected to answer with a meaningful lift of her brow, hoping he'd recall every autocratic tone he'd used with her along the way.

In response, an amused scoff escaped those sensual lips, and he set his paintbrush in the pan, turning to face her. "I warned Nikki taking a spin on her friend's homemade zip line was dangerous," he said. He looked across the water, squinting into the sunshine. But he clearly wasn't focused on the view, his voice reflective. "So she's annoyed my prediction proved accurate. She's angry that she ruined her summer plans. Worse, her only choice was to either move in with my mother at her expensive retirement village with all her cronies, or—"

Jax bit back a smile at the suggestion, and Blake went on. "Exactly," he said drily, apparently agreeing with her unspoken comment as he continued. "Or move in here under the, and I quote, 'tyrannical eye of my big brother.'"

"I guess that's what siblings are for."

"To drive each other crazy?" he said with a skeptical look.

She struggled to keep a straight face. "Yeah. And not that you'd be surprised," she went on, "but when you're not around, Nikki calls you her big brother and her capitalized Big Brother, in the Orwellian sense."

The eyebrow bisected by the tiny scar shot higher in amusement.

"If it's any consolation," she said, "Nikki says you're the guy every law-enforcement officer wants trying their cases. She thinks you're a brilliant lawyer."

The praise seemed to surprise him, and he leaned back against the unpainted part of the rail, crossing his arms. The full-on sight of his beautiful biceps and the shirt stretched across the lightly muscled chest almost sent her into the deep end of the bay. Every atom in her body adjusted to peer in his direction.

Jax cleared her throat. "And given my predicament, her belief in your brilliance is reassuring."

The brain she needed. The brawn was a distraction, begging to be explored.

"I spoke with Sara again this morning," he said, interrupting her mutinous thoughts. "She offered to help with your case. As a former public defender, and a brilliant one at that, she's well qualified to offer advice."

Jax bit back a frown. She was incredibly grateful he was going out of his way to do a good job, but a very tiny part of her was disturbed he was consulting with his perfect other half. But despite the fact that Blake was conferring with the beautiful lawyer, or maybe even because of it, he still deserved Jax's gratitude.

Which was why she'd risked coming to talk to the deliciously disruptive, infinitely touchable man.

"In that case—" taking extra-special care *not* to touch him, she held out her hand for the paintbrush with an appreciative smile "—in thanks for all of your hard work, I'll finish this section while you take a moment to relax."

Wariness flickered through his eyes. As if trying to decide if he wanted her continued company or not, Blake gave a cautious glance down at her waiting hand, which was then followed by a small frown of discovery on his face. His eyes zeroed in on her arm, and her stomach dropped. When he lightly grasped her hand—sending a jolt through her body—and pulled her arm closer to better visualize the tattoo on the inside of her wrist, her stomach rolled…

Oh, hell. Keeping her hands to herself was the least of her worries now.

"I never noticed the scars under your tattoo," he said in a low voice.

The sensation of his hand on her skin combined with the scrutiny of her battle wounds made speaking impossible. Heart pumping hard, she willed herself to remain calm, making sure her voice was light. Or as light as she could manage, anyway. Because one scar could easily be an accident.

Two parallel ones were definitely suspicious.

She fought for a breezy tone, falling just short of the mark. "I didn't try to kill myself, if that's what you're thinking."

"I'm well aware people cut themselves for other reasons," he said.

And the unspoken knowledge in his gaze, the understanding in his expression, set her pulse pounding harder. There was no denying the look on his face. He knew the wounds had been self-inflicted.

He knew she'd once been a cutter.

Her chest seemed to shrink to half its size, trapping the breath in her lungs. It was one thing to come to thank the man for his help. Baring her history to those probing, all-seeing eyes was another. But now that the tumultuous mindset of her adolescent years had been exposed, she refused to offer up excuses or cower meekly in the corner, pretending he'd misunderstood. She curled her fingers against her palm.

Because, damn it, she'd battled those demons—had waged a war against the crippling insecurities of her youth—and *won*.

"It was a long time ago, when I was just a teen," she said simply, hoping he wouldn't interrogate her further. After the Jack fiasco, she wasn't ready for that kind of reveal again. "The parallel marks reminded me of part of a musical staff. So a couple of years ago, I had the extra lines tattooed on and added musical notes."

The lengthy pause was filled with warm sunshine, a salty breeze and the sound of lapping waves and ruffling sails. Jax couldn't move, couldn't think, couldn't *breathe*, dying to hear how he would respond to her admission about the origin of her scars.

Until Blake finally said, "Musical notes to which song?"

Stunned, she leaned back and cocked her hip, staring up at

him. Of all the questions she'd expected, that one had never crossed her mind. Two years ago Jack's disappointing reactions to the marks on her body had inspired the tattoo and choice of song. Since then, no one had ever asked her about her choice. Leave it to the astutely observant Blake to suss out that they weren't just random notes she'd chosen on a whim.

Curious how he'd react to the news, and hugely relieved by the change in topic, she said, "They're the first phrase to Madonna's 'Like a Virgin.'"

A small grunt escaped his lips, a combination of shocked surprise...and amusement.

"You don't approve of my choice?" She fought a smile, struggling to maintain the deadpan face as she went on. "Or maybe you think the song doesn't suit me?"

"I have nothing against Madonna, per se," he said.

He cast an eye over her short shorts and the tank top displaying the local rap artist Bulldog. Blake's assessing look was electrifying, prickling the hair at her neck. Her shirt emphasized her breasts in a way that could hardly be described as modest.

Blake hesitated, as if considering the rest of his answer, and then dropped his gaze back to the arm still cradled in his hand. He lightly touched the line of one scar, and a searing bolt of nerves nearly crippled her body. The simple caress was sensual. Seductive.

Hot.

And as scary as hell as he traced the marks that had come to symbolize the fight to achieve peace with her past. Her warrior wounds were a visible reminder of the inner conflict she'd battled. Profoundly disturbed, she resisted the urge to splay her hand on his hard chest and stroke lower....

Blake ran his finger up one line of puckered skin and back down the other, leaving her body aching with need, her breath frozen in her throat as he finally went on. "But you hardly impress me as the virginal type," he said.

Imagine if he were privy to the unholy thoughts racing through her mind now?

The secret urges ramped her heart rate higher. "So tell me, Suit," she said as lightly as she could. "What exactly is a virgin supposed to act like? An innocent, frightened and confused by the feelings a man stirs when he's near?" She almost rolled her eyes at the ridiculously old-fashioned notion before lifting her brow higher, ignoring her thrumming body. "Or should I be outraged that you have the audacity to touch my chaste skin?" she asked with a wry tone.

She might be a virgin, but she refused to let the technicality define her. She wasn't afraid or confused. And she certainly wasn't outraged.

She was *aroused*.

As if he didn't quite believe her claim, a slow smile of entertainment lifted his lips. "Let's put it this way," he said as his thumb continued to stroke her skin. "The first time we met, you performed a provocative dance to a hip-hop song on the courthouse lawn. The second time we met, you were behind bars." He pursed his lips, his eyes growing dark. "So it's safe to say you haven't exactly been giving off many virginal vibes."

She held his heated gaze, refusing to acknowledge the heady feel of his thumb against her wrist, the wild longing to return the caress. But the slight part of her mouth as she fought for air must have given her away.

Because his words came out rough. "And you're definitely not giving off virginal vibes now."

His gaze briefly moved down to the rapid rise and fall of her breasts, and then back to her face, gray eyes radiating an intensity that had had her on edge from the moment they'd met. She could read everything. The hesitation. The hint of wariness. But, most important, the frank desire. And then his gaze settled on her lips, weakening her resolve not to touch him.

The heat from the hand that cupped her arm spread to

every corner of her body, concentrating in her most sensitized parts. Leaving her feeling soft. Compliant. And damp.

Melting her resolve to thank him and bolt, *before* she did something stupid.

"I can see you're thinking about kissing me—" Jax said, the words breaking at a slight catch in her voice. "But I know you well enough by now to realize you won't go through with it."

"What makes you think I won't?" he said.

"Because you're far too disciplined to let your lust run away with your emotions."

Although the heat in his eyes seared her to the soul, he said, "Agreed."

The flash of disappointment slashed deep. "Too bad."

And while his agreement wasn't a surprise, that didn't make the words any easier to hear. She had wants. *Needs.* Like the overwhelming desire to drive a man to distraction, despite the marks on her body, the visual reminders of her past. The hope that someone, someday, would lose his head over Jacqueline Lee, scars and all. Instituting a temporary embargo on men hadn't been easy, even after Jack's defection. But she'd never met anyone quite like Blake.

And if making love to him out, then she at least deserved a kiss.

Finally abandoning the vow to keep her hands to herself—a hopeless goal, in retrospect—she reached up with her free arm and clutched his shirt, knuckles pressed against his hard chest. Blake allowed her to pull him closer. Which was a good thing, because with their height difference, without that little bit of cooperation she'd never reach his mouth.

And if one kiss was all she was gonna get, then she intended to make damn sure it was a good one....

The attraction that had slammed into him the day they'd met, the fierce need that repeatedly brought him to his figurative knees, returned with a vigor that stunned Blake with its intensity. The moment Jax's hand had landed on his chest, time had contracted, becoming more vivid and defined, his world reduced to the sensory input of the beautiful woman. He was mesmerized by her wild tawny hair and the seductive hazel eyes. Captivated by the insistent hand against his chest and the soft skin of her arm beneath his fingers.

Troubled by the raised scars beneath his thumb.

Heart thumping, he absently traced the well-healed marks, fighting his overworked libido as his mind furiously grappled with the physical proof that, at one time, Jax hadn't been the strong, to-hell-with-the-world woman that stood before him now. In light of her history, he wasn't surprised her adolescent years had been fraught with the occasional destructive behavior. But it was a true testament to her amazing resilience that the self-harming had been limited to the two scars—the rest of her arms and legs were silky smooth and scar-free. No wonder she cultivated a carpe diem attitude and longed to feel like a virgin again, untouched. Innocent. And free from the weight of her past. He'd never met such a complicated woman.

And those complexities made her all that more attractive.

Heat coursed through his body as her gaze radiated a come-hither look mixed with an emotional honesty that had enchanted him from the moment they'd met. Knowing his arguments were growing weaker by the minute, he mentally listed them anyway. She wasn't his type. She didn't fit with his life, because, between the Menendez case and his sister, life was too full already. And Jax was pure trouble, the hellion on heels a walking, talking disaster on the move. Which didn't mean he couldn't sleep with her, but it absolutely meant that he *shouldn't*.

But, try as he might, Blake couldn't pull his gaze from the delicate part of her lips or stop his thumb from tracing her scars. But he'd be damned before he'd let his fascination with the woman seduce him, or let his lust dictate whom he slept with—

Jax rose up on her toes and placed her mouth on his lips.

Paralyzed, Blake fought the need to crush her supple body against his, concentrating on the taste of caramel. The smell of citrus from her hair. The soft skin now gripped firmly in his hand, covering the tattoo that was wholly inappropriate.

Because there was nothing virginal about the way Jax was kissing him. It was the kiss of a woman who knew what she was doing. And knew what she wanted, as well.

His heart pounded harder as she moved her mouth with a purpose, parting her lips just enough to tease him with the promise of more heat. The teasing hint of her tongue. Kisses that were warm and moist and soft and steeped in the unique flavor of Jax. His body craved more, and he slanted his head a bit, allowing her slightly better access.

Jax melted against him, full breasts plastered against his chest as her tongue took a bolder taste of his, demanding he reciprocate.

Pulse throbbing, he grew hard, making restraint difficult to maintain as he indulged in a mind-boggling erotic fantasy. Blake's brain swirled with images of him walking her backward into the cabin of his boat, stripping her out of her clothes, pinning her tattoo-adorned arm over her head and burying himself between those toned, tanned legs. Consuming her in every way imaginable.

She wouldn't say no, but would embrace the act of making love just like she embraced everything else about life. Wholeheartedly. Without reservation. And with a passion that would be impossible to forget.

Her lips moved against his in an act that grew more insistent, more impossible to resist as time wore on, calling to him. Weakening his good sense. Until he knew if he didn't put an end to the kiss, he *would* make love to her. Right here.

And right now…

CHAPTER FIVE

WITH A SILENT curse and a loud protest from his raging libido, Blake gripped Jax's shoulders and gently but firmly set her back.

Whoops and cheers and a shout of "Go, Ms. Lee" came from the distance, and Blake glanced up to see the two guitar students watching them from the pool deck, clearly delighted by the scene.

Chest still heaving, Jax stared up at him, gaze hot, and said, "Did I scare you, Suit?"

Her sassy words shoved him closer to the edge.

"No," he said, his voice disconcertingly gruff.

If he were smart, he'd be afraid. But fear wasn't the reason for the adrenaline careening through his veins. No, the current wild surge of blood was in response to a need that threatened to be his undoing. And despite the desire that still raged, his brow crinkled in resigned amusement.

"But I hope that demonstration wasn't another one of those life lessons for your students," he said, and she narrowed her eyes at him.

Lips pressed in a determined line, fighting both a smile and the urge to take her feisty, luscious mouth again, Blake turned back to the rail and picked up his brush.

She'd kissed him.

A week later and her mind still churned from the interlude, so Jax leaned back against the chaise longue and tried to relax. The turquoise waters of the pool stretched out at her feet, the waterfall gurgling nearby. And beyond the deck on the far side, the surface of the bay sparkled in the sun. Nikki was sitting at a patio table reading while her mother fixed sandwiches for lunch and prepared a homemade apple pie—a new recipe Abigail Bennington wanted to try after her week away at a cooking institute. The smell was unusual. Nikki had warned Jax to insist on a small slice, and Abigail had feigned outrage at the indirect insult. Jax found the two women endearing.

So she should feel at ease and relaxed. But she wasn't. Because she'd kissed Blake and he hadn't kissed her back. Okay, so he hadn't pushed her away exactly, but his participation had been minimal. And if that wasn't enough of an ego thrasher, he'd been avoiding her ever since.

In the past week, only twice had he made it home from the office in time for dinner.

Jax had stayed busy with Nikki, the brunette helping her kick-start a phone campaign searching for donors for the club. They'd also managed a short shopping excursion and an afternoon at the beach, Nikki's red bikini matching her dragon cast tattoo. Today Jax had driven Nikki to the doctor, who'd declared she had at least three more weeks in the cast. But even one more day spent being avoided by Blake felt like torture.

All thanks to the constant flame burning in her body since The Kiss.

A spark that refused to die.

Considering she'd made a vow to be strong until she found someone who was right for her—someone who didn't consider Jacqueline Lee a *total* loon—she should be grateful Blake had the ability to control what she couldn't.

From behind her, Nikki called out in greeting. "Blake, my long-lost big bro."

Jax's heart surged, but she refused to turn and watch him

approach, dreading seeing him again. Disgusted with the cowardly thoughts, Jax flopped over onto her stomach and buried her head in her crossed arms.

Right now, she wasn't sure what annoyed her more, her ambivalent feelings about his appearance, or his cool control. Was he here simply to torture her? To rub her face in the knowledge that she had made a pass at him and he'd pushed her away? On edge, and unable to lie still now that he was present, Jax rose and dived into the pool.

A jolt of cool water closed around her overheated body, giving her the shock she needed, clearing her head. She set off across the pool, freestyle.

Of course he hadn't come to see her. He was here to eat lunch with his mother and sister, to check up on his family because he was a no-nonsense kinda guy who believed in responsibility. Duties. Sane, rational decisions. And since Mr. Self-Control's will was so strong, she should use that in her favor. After several laps, her muscles fatigued from the work, she'd finally calmed a bit. Maybe she was ready to face him now?

But Blake saved her the trouble of deciding.

On her last lap, she broke the surface of the water and looked up to find him staring down at her, suit coat unbuttoned to reveal a blue dress shirt and lean hips, her beach towel in his hand.

"Enjoying the water?" he said from above.

"I was," she said, with meaningful emphasis on the second word. She dropped her gaze and crossed her arms on the pool edge, taking comfort in the warm tile and the less disturbing sight of his expensive-looking black leather shoes.

His knees came into view as he squatted down, the muscles in his legs bunching, stretching the crease in those perfectly pressed trousers.

Everything about the man was perfectly pressed, including his libido.

Irritation surged. "Aren't you afraid you'll ruin your suit so close to the pool?"

"Not at all." A small lift of his broad shoulders came and went. "It's just a suit."

"If you can afford to pay too much for your clothes, only to treat them so cavalierly, surely you can afford your own towel." She nodded her head toward his hand closed around the fabric. "That one's mine."

He glanced at the cloth he clutched. "I'm aware of that. The picture of The Doors was a dead giveaway." Holding it out, he hiked an eyebrow expectantly. "I'm bringing it to you."

Her brain buzzed at his proximity and the sensual awareness in his eyes. She bit her lip, wishing she hadn't chosen the one-piece swimsuit that showed off her cleavage. "How kind," she said, not meaning the words. "But it's arrogant of you to assume I'm finished with my swim."

Lips twitching, he steadily held her gaze and didn't move. "Lunch is ready."

Obviously, he wanted her to get out of the pool.

Frowning, her stomach in turmoil, she pressed her lips flat. The swim had been a waste. An eternity wouldn't be long enough to face Blake across the table in a bathing suit.

"I'm not hungry yet," she said.

"Trust me," he said drily. "Eating my mother's food has little to do with hunger. In my house, it's a duty."

"Well, then," she said, sending a forced, brilliantly false smile up at him. "I know you are a very busy and very important man. With so many criminals to lock up and all. So please, feel free to get started without me."

His head dipped a fraction to the right. Was that a challenge she saw in his eyes? The tone of his voice affirmed the answer to the question.

"You wouldn't want your food to get cold," he said, his eyes intense.

With the way he was looking at her, even the coming of

a second ice age would prevent her food from getting cold. And how could he gaze at her like that? As if he wanted her but still had the power to control it. To walk away.

Damn it. A week ago he *had* walked away.

"It's chicken salad," she said. "It's supposed to be cold."

A ghost of a grin came and went on those sexy lips, leaving her heart knocking harder in her chest. Shoot. Why was she so susceptible to the rare sighting of one of his smiles?

Perhaps because they did beautiful things to his handsome face.

He glanced up at the cloudless sky, the powder-blue brilliant in the midday sun. "Very well," he said with a patient tone. The kind that communicated a steely reserve that brooked no concession of wills. "You wouldn't want your chicken salad to get hot."

The jumble of nerves knotted in her stomach pulled tighter, and Jax swallowed hard, her mouth set. "You're not going to go away until I get out of this pool, are you?"

The gray eyes assessing hers from above sparked like flint on steel, and glowed, rivaling the sun. "No," he said as he stood, lowering his free hand toward her. "I'm not."

The knocking in her chest grew more insistent as Jax clutched the pool ledge. Gripping her lower lip between her teeth, she placed her palm in his. The strong hand around hers left her lungs hungry for breath, her body wanting more of his touch. She braced her foot on the pool wall, and Blake lifted her effortlessly.

Standing beside him, water rushed down her skin and pooled at her feet. Her one-piece gently cupped her breasts, emphasizing the curves. And even though the cut was relatively modest by today's standards, his perusal made her feel naked. Exposed. And the last time she'd stood exposed in front of man, her body completely bared before Jack, he'd looked at her in horror.

She laid a soothing hand on her belly and bit back the awful memory that killed her libido.

But Blake's colorless eyes swept down her body and back, resurrecting the thrill. His expression was neutral, but his eyes burned brighter than ever. "Nice suit."

She pulled her towel from his hand. "There's no need to check up on me," she said. She swiped the towel down her trunk, annoyed that she felt flustered. "I'd hate to put a crimp in your schedule."

Forehead lined with a mixture of amusement and feigned surprise, Blake said, "You seemed fairly eager for my company last week."

"I'll plead the Fifth Amendment."

"I think an insanity plea might be more fitting."

"For my actions? Or for yours?"

"Both, I suspect." Though simmering with a latent heat, his intense eyes were extraordinarily steady as he studied her. "Regardless, why are you in such a big hurry to get rid of me today?"

Because she wanted him with an intensity that was embarrassing.

"Unexpected change of heart." Fingers fumbling with nerves, it took several attempts to successfully knot the towel at her waist. "It's a woman's prerogative to change her mind. So…" She waved a hand in the air, as if he were a stray cat she could shoo away. "You can get back to your work now." Parking the hand on her hip, she added, "No need to stay."

His lips quirked in humor. "But I'm hungry. I worked up an appetite formulating my defense strategy to keep you from getting locked away."

He turned and placed a hand on her arm, eliciting a zing of sultry sensations as he propelled her toward the table. Steam had to be rising from her skin.

"Besides, Ms. Lee," he said smoothly, "there's a rather significant problem with your change of heart."

"What's that?"

If he hadn't been steadying her, Jax would have tripped when he said, "Apparently I've grown addicted to your company."

At a quarter to midnight, Blake upped the speed on the treadmill in his exercise room, his feet pounding out his frustration and the pent-up sexual energy. Sweat clung to his body as he deliberately ignored the knowledge that Jax slept in his guest cottage.

Despite being five miles beyond his usual goal, he wasn't near ready to end his punishing run. The memory of her lovely hips in a bathing suit drove his relentless pace. The remembered sight of her breasts so seductively displayed pushed him harder. But it was her heated gaze in response to his addiction confession that compelled him to keep going.

Lips set grimly, he turned up the speed and stretched his legs farther, eating up more of the nonexistent miles as he pushed himself, his muscles howling in protest. In truth, he had no one to blame but himself, since today he'd been the one to seek *her* out...all because the grueling pace of his life was starting to wear him down.

The stifling fist of responsibility tightened its grip in his chest.

The pace he'd set for himself at work and keeping Nikki out of trouble—and fixing the mess when she *did*—were taking a toll, sapping all hope for relaxation. So far, Jax had been the busiest, most delicious complication precipitated by his little sister to date. But he'd made the rare appearance at lunch today because he'd suddenly felt the need for a little levity. The kind of lightness and good humor that Jax always provided.

Even when she was being a total pain.

But the double-edged sword cut deep, her presence reminding him of how she'd taken him with her eyes and her mouth on his boat, triggering fantasies of her in his bed. He hadn't been able to banish the treacherous visions since they'd first arrived, threatening his sanity.

Visions of Jax opening beneath him.

Visions of her body arching to accept his.

Burning with frustration, he stabbed the off button on the treadmill and hopped off, heading down the hall and into his bedroom, not bothering to turn on the light. Maybe a cold shower would ease the fiery need. But when he paused at the window, the lights from the guest cottage reached out to him in the dark night.

Jax wasn't asleep. She was awake.

Hand fisted tight, he braced his arm against the window, the war being waged within growing fierce. The battle bloody. He could no more deny his need for Jax than he could change all the circumstances that made a relationship with her a massive mistake. Which meant it was time to admit what he'd been fighting all along: sex with Jax was unavoidable.

A frown crossed his face. Sleeping with her might be a given, but the event would have to wait until *after* he was done with the Menendez case. He couldn't afford any distractions. Too much was riding on his success.

Sweat trickled down his back, cooling his body in the air-conditioning, but the fire that burned for Jax refused to die. And waiting even five more minutes to taste the reckless woman seemed too much to ask.

A shadow passed by a window in the cottage, and Blake's heart pumped faster.

Chest heaving, he hated that even a vague sighting of her left him champing at the bit, his body straining and growing hard. Insisting on satisfaction.

Burning for release.

With a muttered curse, Blake closed his eyes and gave in, his hand sliding beneath the waistband of his shorts, closing around the part of him that would not be denied. And, picturing Jax's smoky gaze and that bold, sassy mouth, Blake gave in to the need.

At midnight, Jax finally heaved out a breath and flopped onto the leather couch in the guest cottage, hot tea in hand. The luxurious accommodations consisted of a sitting area, kitchen, bedroom and a beautiful marble bathroom. The living room allowed her plenty of room to pace as she pondered the problem of bringing the public's attention to the club, but her mind refused to focus.

Because Blake surely hadn't acted like a man addicted to her company.

Jax sighed and leaned her head back. Lunch with Blake's family had included a discussion about Jax's first court appearance tomorrow afternoon. Hardly a reassuring topic. And then, once the meal was over, Blake had gone back to work and hadn't come home for dinner. How was that for a man supposedly craving her presence? So Jax had watched a bit of TV, alone, and the eleven-o'clock news included a piece on the Menendez drug-cartel case, with a brief clip of a reporter interviewing the lead prosecuting attorney... Blake Bennington.

The sight of the coolly collected man had just about sent her body into a tizzy. The oh-so smoothly articulate Blake, looking *GQ* fine in his suit and coverworthy handsome face, answered the reporter's questions with an authority that few would dare question. If he handled himself in the courtroom half as well as he'd handled the interview, her legal problems would be well taken care of.

Which meant, hopefully, her return to her old life would work out. *If* she could secure the money to get the music program up and running again, of course.

Her heart nose-dived at the thought.

The flash mob had been her first attempt to raise awareness, but public interest had faded fast. And so far the phone campaign hadn't brought in nearly enough. To top it all off, she wondered if her failure to come up with a better plan was somehow related to being distracted, her mind constantly occupied with thoughts of Blake. One more sex dream about the man and she might remain happily catatonic for life, living out her fantasies in her head.

And the advantages of remaining conscious were slipping fast.

Unnerved and restless, Jax looked out the window, the lights in Blake's bedroom twinkling through the swaying palms. Apparently Mr. Workaholic had finally arrived home. Sipping her tea, she wondered what he was up to now. More work? Getting ready for bed? And would he be in boxers or briefs?

Blood singing at the thought, she downed the rest of her tea and set the mug on the coffee table with a thunk.

Enough, Jax. The state of his underwear isn't your concern. The lack of funding for the club is.

Spying her guitar, she crossed the living room and picked it up. Music always made her feel better, helped her think. She would play a little, relax and come up with another idea to obtain the funds. She just needed to get her mind off the man who held her fate in his hands and her body at the mercy of her steamy thoughts.

Music and the sound of soothing waves should do the trick.

Guitar in hand, she pushed through the front door and settled into a chaise longue on the teak deck facing Biscayne Bay and the city beyond. The moon and the twinkling lights of Miami offered the only light, and Jax was glad the cottage blocked the view of Blake's house. She crossed her legs, settling the guitar across her thighs. But indecision gripped her, and she started—and stopped—several songs in rapid succession, feeling too melancholy for rock and roll. Not melancholy enough for the blues. Nothing seemed to fit her mood.

Her lips twisted in contemplation, and she was just about to strum the first chord to a good butt-kicking country song when a voice cut the air.

"You're up late."

At the sound of Blake's voice, her heart jumped and desire clamped around her body. Jax briefly closed her eyes.

You're a warrior, Jax. Be strong.

She spoke without looking at him. "Says the man who got home from work at midnight." A brief moment of dreaded guilt racked her. "When I asked you to help me with my legal problem, I had no idea you were the lead prosecutor in the Menendez case."

Blake finally came into view, stopping at the deck railing in front of her. The full moon outlined his form. The only concession to the time of day was the lack of a jacket and tie.

Unbelievable. Midnight...and the man was *still* wearing a dress shirt and pants.

"The trial has been all over the news," she said. "No wonder you're away from home so much."

Jeez, she hoped she didn't sound like a petulant kid.

He leaned against the railing. "It's taken a lot of work to get to this point," he said simply. "Previous efforts to nail Menendez have been unsuccessful."

Jax studied him for a moment. Though easy, the tone in his voice brooked no argument: Blake Bennington was going to bring down this guy. It was the same determination he'd exhibited on the news clip, only it was a thousand times stronger in person. So maybe his absence from home was less about avoiding her and more about his drive.

And suddenly, she wanted to know why he drove himself so hard. Why he spent so much of his life dedicating himself to his job. Away from his home. Away from his family. And away from *her*.

Because if *that* was the reason she was going to miss out on the experience of a lifetime, she wanted to know.

Curious, she tipped her head. "Is this the biggest case you've worked on?"

"It's the most important one," he said.

"Because it's so high-profile?"

"High-profile is nice because that leads to the potential for promotion."

She paused, digesting the information. "Surely you're not dedicating all this work time simply in the name of upward mobility."

Something in the set of his chin, the tension in his body, told her that wasn't the only reason why he was living and breathing this case.

She pushed on. "Why else is it important?"

Several seconds passed before he responded, as if deciding just how much to share, and then Blake finally leaned his elbow against the rail. From his posture she knew the answer would be worth paying close attention to.

"Ten years ago my father was killed in a car accident," he said evenly. The words weren't what she was expecting, and her body went still as he went on. "The driver that hit Dad's vehicle was strung out on cocaine sold to him by a dealer just like the one in Menendez's organization."

Her throat grew tight. Nikki had mentioned their father's car accident, but not the cause. And the loss of a parent to such a senseless act seemed so unfair. Of course, when it came to losing family, Jax was well versed in the unfairness of the universe. But if there were any emotions churning inside Blake, his steady demeanor masked them well.

"So every case that brings down a piece of one of these organizations feels like a particularly sweet victory," he said.

"I'm sorry," she said, knowing the words were horribly inadequate.

Blake shrugged, as if the sympathy was unnecessary. "It was a long time ago," he said. "Nikki was only twelve."

Twelve. A preteen.

A ribbon of moonlight rippled on the bay, and Jax stared at his boat gently rocking in the warm, nighttime breeze, small waves lapping a seductive rhythm against the hull. In the time since she'd been here, she'd only seen the man do maintenance on the boat. Not once had he taken it out on the water. His father's death explained a lot about his driving dedication to his job, as well as the siblings' complicated relationship—Blake assuming the role of both brother and father figure. And suddenly his overdeveloped sense of responsibility made sense.

As did the frustratingly logical side that won over his own needs, the *passion*.

Every. Single. Time.

Her curiosity about the man grew tenfold, including a desire to know if he ever let loose and enjoyed himself.

"So tell me, Suit." She nodded in the direction of his dock. "Every Sunday you tend to your catamaran, but when was the last time you actually took your boat on a trip?"

When Blake went still, Jax was sure the question had hit a nerve.

CHAPTER SIX

THOUGH HE TENSED at the question, Blake propped a hip against the rail, concentrating on the salty air and the form of the woman sitting cross-legged and barefoot on the chaise longue. She'd set the guitar aside and was now studying him closely. Tonight, all of his efforts to stay away had failed.

And, man, those efforts had been *extensive*....

He'd heard the music and stepped outside for a little fresh air, promising himself he'd simply enjoy her entertaining company for a moment. Blake's lips twisted at the picture of the Rolling Stones displayed on her top. And one look at the rest of Jax made pretense impossible. Tearing himself away would be tough. Her hair was loose and hanging wildly down her back, the fantasy-inducing legs bared beneath her simple knit shorts and matching short-sleeved shirt. An outfit that, on closer inspection, looked more like pajamas.

He was in serious trouble.

Blake forced himself to focus, despite the disturbing turn in the conversation. "Other than the occasional maintenance run, I haven't taken the boat on an overnight trip since my father died."

Her wincing frown was instantaneous. "*Jeez*, Blake." She unfolded her legs, leaning forward with an earnest look, and he was struck by the realization it was the first time she'd called him by his name. "Your family is right. You need to learn to relax more." He frowned and considered protesting, but she went on. "I saw you on TV today," she said. "You played your part well, that of the confident attorney out to get his man." She tipped her head skeptically. "But is that all you want out of life?"

He didn't answer, the words burning through him.

She stood, crossing to stand in front of him. "Look, I know how hard it is to lose a parent," she said, and the understanding in her eyes made his heart cinch.

She'd suffered so many losses.

But it wasn't just the loss that was eating at him. It was the attempt to live up to his obligations and keep the promises he'd made to his father before he'd died. Struggling to walk in his father's shoes, day by day. And those shoes were feeling tighter and tighter as time went by. For once Blake wanted to chuck the responsibility and do what *he* wanted. Like making love to Jax.

Because he wanted her with an ache that couldn't be appeased by his own hand.

She shot him a concerned look. "But you can't let that one tragedy ruin your life twice." Her gaze was earnest. "You have to bounce better than that."

He bit back a smile, amused by her chastising words, and he was suddenly overcome with the need to touch her...so he shoved his hands in his pockets.

She must have read his mind because, when their gazes met and held, the moment was filled with more than just two people discussing their priorities in life. It was filled with an awareness of the promise in their aborted kiss, and his body tightened in response.

"Your hair is damp at the ends," she said softly.

Hell, don't look at me like that, Jax.

His voice sounded too husky. "I ran on the treadmill when I got home and needed a shower."

But he'd needed the shower for more reasons than just the one....

"And yet you couldn't throw on a pair of shorts?" she said.

He hoped his tone masked his growing tension. "These were handy."

Because when he'd heard her guitar, he'd been in too much of a hurry, grabbing the closest items.

"Well, you're not in the courtroom, Suit," she said, stepping forward to touch the collar of his shirt, and his heart tripped and landed with a jolt. "If you don't have time for your boat, you can at least relax and unbutton more than just the top button."

The tangle of desire, the one that had permanently set up residence in his gut since meeting Jax, unfurled, twining tenaciously around his every cell.

The warm sea breeze carried the scent of strawberries, and her proximity made logic impossible, his chest tight. He wanted the woman who took life by storm. He wanted the woman who planted unvirgin-like kisses on a man who'd passed on every chance to kiss a woman for six months. Until Jax. He wanted Jax and...

That was all. He wanted Jax.

And he wasn't strong enough to wait.

Decision made, hands still in his pockets, Blake maintained her gaze as the hum of awareness buzzed louder in his head, drowning out any lingering doubts.

His voice was gruffer than he'd planned. "Why don't you take my shirt off for me?"

The full moon lit the desire that flared in her eyes, sending an explosion of heat ricocheting through his body. It was almost a relief to meet the expectant air head-on. Blake concentrated on the feel of Jax absently rubbing the silk collar, the way she was looking at him melting him from the inside out. Their kiss on the boat hung in the air between them like unfinished business. Everything about their relationship felt like unfinished business. The attraction in the limo. Jax perched on his desk and driving him mad with want. In his car, touching his mouth. And then, of course, there was today by the pool.

And each time had twisted Blake's need tighter. Despite his earlier efforts, he feared one touch would release the pent-up energy and send him spinning out of control.

Jax lifted a brow with a look that was almost a reprimand. "Is kissing allowed now?" she asked. She took a step closer, and her voice dropped. "Because you need to make up your mind and be consistent. Otherwise I can't keep up with all of your rules."

Heart tripping faster than he'd thought possible, he looked down at her, fighting the need to jerk her into his arms. Elbows tight by his sides. Hands burrowed in his pockets. The Rolling Stones logo stretched across the tempting expanse of her left breast, making resistance difficult to maintain.

"Since when do you care about rules?" he said.

"I don't," she said, fingers toying with his top button. "I'm just trying to keep up with your ridiculous list." She stared at him, her eyes scorching. "So why don't you tell me what's on your mind."

The look on her face was all fire and heat, while his libido strained on his self-imposed leash. Every molecule in his body had been preoccupied with thoughts of taking her since his fingers had first closed around her wrist in the limo. And take her he would, but they had a few things to discuss first.

Heart pumping hard in anticipation, he laid out all the internal arguments he'd been wrestling with since the moment they'd met. "I never sleep with women I'm involved with professionally. And before I enter any relationship, I give it careful consideration. I think long and hard about compatibility." God knew he couldn't afford another woman in his life that needed bailing out of trouble. He needed someone sensible. *Rational.* "That usually requires a three-month getting-to-know-you period. And…" He paused for effect and held her gaze, needing to lay out his case very clearly. If he was going to be selfish, he needed her to know where he was coming from. "And I don't do one-night stands."

The disappointment in her face was almost his undoing. Apparently, she thought he was about to push her away again.

"Impressive list," she said. "Which just about describes everything I'm not. So why are you telling me all this?"

"Because I want to be clear where I'm coming from before I spend tonight making you the single exception to all of those rules."

Gaze locked on his, Jax blinked, her fingers frozen on his shirt. "When did you come to this decision?"

"Fifteen minutes ago."

"That long, huh?" She lifted an amused brow. "Logical thinking doesn't come as naturally to me as it apparently does to you," she said, and then she popped the second button of his shirt open, sending a crippling surge of pleasure through his body.

Blake gripped her hips, his fingers splayed along her backside, his tone rough. "I'll take that as consent."

"It'd be pretty dense of you if you didn't."

Hands clutching her gentle curves, he walked her backward and trapped her against the cottage door. With one more step, he brought them flush, his erection pressed just above the V at her thighs, and he bit back the groan of pleasure.

Soon.

Need coursed through him, but he'd be damned if he'd come unglued now. Never mind that it had been months since he'd last touched a woman. And it didn't matter that this was Jax, the woman who had him so twisted in knots he feared he'd never untangle his emotions.

He was going to do this right.

"There's something I've wanted to do to you since that day in the limo," Jax said.

Blake went still, ready to patiently enjoy any and all activities the beautiful lady had planned. "Feel free to do whatever you'd like, Ms. Lee," Blake murmured, fingers biting into her hips.

She arched an eyebrow coyly. "Whatever?"

The thrill almost brought him to his knees. "Whatever."

A sly grin stretched across her face as she lifted her hands to his head, threading her fingers through his hair, gently mussing the strands.

A look of satisfaction settled on her face. "It was a long time in coming, but it's been well worth the wait."

"Messing up my hair?" he asked incredulously.

"The rumpled look goes well with your midnight shadow," she said, rubbing her soft palms against the stubble on his chin.

When she dropped her hands down to his arms, he said, "Is that all?"

A quick flash of hurt and confusion flitted through her eyes, and Blake suddenly felt like a bastard.

But she hiked that stubborn chin. "I don't want to be responsible for making you lose all that careful control of yours," she said with a lofty air. Sliding her hands to his chest, her secretive grin returned as she began to release more buttons on his shirt. "You might end up hurting yourself."

"You don't frighten me."

Jax cocked her head, her fingers working her way lower. "Should I be offended?"

"Absolutely not."

Her hands reached the buttons at his abdomen, her knuckles brushing his skin, and his gut clenched in fierce anticipation.

Hoping his fingers weren't digging too deep into the soft flesh of her hips, Blake breathed in her scent, wishing she'd go faster. And needing to remind her about his cuffs. "Jax—"

"Don't interrupt my concentration," she said.

Her fingers fumbled a little as she struggled to pop the bottom buttons, her hands near the erection that was clearly outlined beneath his pants. A small line formed between her eyebrows as she focused on her task.

Blake's heart twisted at the adorable look on her face. This was no artful seduction. There was no sophistication in her movements. Beneath the teasing humor, he could pick up on her tension.

Sassy, spunky Jacqueline Lee was nervous.

And knowing she felt out of her league seducing him was a surprise.

Pulling out the tail of his shirt, she clamped her teeth on her lower lip and tugged his shirt down behind his back. When the shirtsleeves got stuck on his wrists, buttons firmly in place, a short gasp of disbelief escaped her lips.

The small sound, combined with the look of total frustration on her face, was endearing, and a low chuckle escaped his lips. "I tried to warn you to unbutton the cuffs."

Her brow furrowed in frustration as she pulled harder, as if through sheer force of will she could overcome her mistake. A typical Jax response to an obstacle.

"Clearly you need a little more practice undressing a man," he said.

"Shut up, Suit," she said lightly.

Hands pinned behind his hips as thoroughly as if he were in shackles, another chuckle escaped Blake. "For future reference, I hear they make special equipment for this," Blake murmured huskily. "Matter of fact, all future ex-cons should be fairly familiar with them."

Her movements stalled and she lifted a brow. "Are you teasing me?"

He bit back a smile. "Of course not."

"Oh, I think you are."

Amused, Blake nodded in the direction of his hands. "Are you going to release me?"

She looked up at him with a mischievous glint in her eyes. "This wasn't part of my plan, but then you laughed at me. Now I'm kinda enjoying it." She placed her palms on his bared chest, and he sucked in a breath. "And I have a strong urge to make you pay for mocking me."

Jax threaded her fingers through the sprinkling of chest hair and then rubbed her palms on his skin, lighting a fire beneath. "Nicely defined muscles," she said. Her hands shifted lower. "Flat stomach." She shot him a look. "You've been making good use of that gym equipment of yours."

Jax touched her mouth to his collarbone, and the explosive shot to his groin ripped a hiss from his lips. Need now outgrowing his patience, Blake pressed his shaft against her soft abdomen and almost groaned in relief, pressing her more firmly against the wall while he breathed in the sweet smell of strawberries.

"You smell like a fresh breeze," she said. Closing his eyes, he basked in the pleasure of her mouth on his skin, her lips moving toward the center of his chest. "But you taste like warm, salty butter," she whispered, pressing small kisses along the top of a pectoral.

His movements restricted by the tight cuffs at his wrists, Blake pulled at the confinement. "Jax," Blake muttered, his voice laced with a husky, barely restrained impatience.

She ignored him and ran her hands up and down his biceps. The faraway look in her eyes and the obvious pleasure on her face ratcheted his lust higher.

"You feel so good," she said, her tone distracted as she trailed her mouth to the other side of his chest. When she reached between them for his belt, the needy feeling grew more urgent, and he began to fear his ability to control the moment was fast slipping from his hands.

His voice was a little harsher now. "Jax," he said, instinct driving him to arch his hips urgently against hers. "I want to touch you." Tipping his head back, he took in her flushed cheeks and the unfocused look as she released the catch on the buckle and pulled the leather strap free.

She lowered her mouth back to his chest. "In a minute," she murmured distractedly against his skin. "I'm not done yet." Moving her hands to the front of his pants, she popped the button and lowered the zipper, knuckles sliding along his erection.

Bolts of lightning skewered his groin. "Damn it, Jax," Blake groaned hoarsely, his pinned arms straining as the electrical shock awoke a powerful need. "Help me get this shirt off."

For months no woman had tempted him to take the time. But Jax proved the exception as he'd watched her wild hair swing behind her back. The lissome sway of her hips as she walked. Her ever-changing scent. The palpable attraction. And right now, if his hands were free, he could touch the woman he needed more than he should.

His tone was harsh. "Jax, please…"

Frustration built as she ignored him, her tongue joining her lips on his chest, her small moan whispering across his damp skin as she pushed his pants down and they dropped around his ankles.

Sweat dotted his temples, his heart banging, and he gritted his teeth.

But the end of his patience soon came.

Her soft fingers encircled his erection and pulled the straining shaft from his briefs, her lips closing around his nipple at the same time, and the fierce stab of dual pleasure was too much.

With a deep growl and a desperate exertion of muscles, the buttons on his cuffs popped, pinging against the deck as his arms finally came free.

Cursing, Blake pushed her right knee up against the wall, using his free hand to sweep the crotch of her knit pants and undies to the side. With a harsh groan and a fearsome thrust that marked the collapse of his control, he buried himself inside her.

"Blake!" she called out, clutching his shoulders.

Heart thundering, he battled for a return to sanity, yet her sex was unbelievably tight. Hot. And oh-so slick. But he needed to stop. He needed to get a grip.

To think logically about—

"Blake," she whispered as she gripped his shoulders, gently rolling her hips as if desperate for more, and desire crushed his fight for restraint.

He pulled back and drove into her again. His breathing harsh, his body quaking with need, he closed his eyes, straining to regain his composure. Praying he could recover his mind and bring her to completion with him. But with every thrust of his hips, pleasure roared through him, and he almost came. The impossibly tight glove of her body, the satisfying pressure, was an agony of the most blissful kind.

"Jax." His gasp for breath was loud as his mind spun to regain footing. "We need a condom," he groaned. "We need to take this to the bedroom."

But Jax rolled her hips again, and her muffled cry of desire speared him with a thrilling satisfaction. Despite his attempt to regain control, the terrible need won out, and he hiked her leg higher, pulled back...and buried himself to the hilt.

A sharp gasp of what sounded like pain escaped Jax's lips, and Blake's eyes flew open.

Eyes closed, Jax clung to his shoulders. "Don't. Move."

It was the look on her face and the strained ache in her voice that finally penetrated his sex-muddled brain as, one by one, the clues slowly congealed into a single earth-shattering reality. When he glanced down at their joined bodies, the evidence was overwhelming, and the shocking realization momentarily paralyzed him. Because Jacqueline "Jax" Lee wasn't just sporting the 'Like a Virgin' tattoo.

She was—up until the moment Blake had lost his hold on sanity—living the life of one, as well.

"Damn it, Jax. I'm sorry," Blake said hoarsely, withdrawing and setting her back on her shaky feet, her body throbbing with intense pleasure and the lingering sting of pain.

Though his hands steadied her, the sudden loss of contact was disorienting, and Jax struggled to comprehend the shocked look on Blake's face.

But his words made his distress clear.

His expression dumbfounded, he said, "Why didn't you tell me?"

"I thought I did."

He plowed a hand through his hair. "Your tattoo suggested that you *feel* like a virgin, not that you *are* one."

The distraught look on his face was almost as bad as Jack's when he'd first attempted to make love to her. And if Blake was this upset about her previous virginal state, imagine how he'd react when he learned the complete truth about her past....

She swallowed hard, struggling for composure. "Can you excuse me for a moment?"

And then, with all the dignity she could muster, she entered the cottage and padded down the hallway, not stopping until she was in the bathroom. Jax closed the door and locked it, her heart pounding.

It was official—Blake must think she was a raving lunatic.

Forcing herself not to hyperventilate, hands clumsy, she shed her pajamas and turned on the hot water in the shower. She stepped into the spray, trying *not* to picture the confounded look on Blake's face. She steadied herself against the wall and let the warm water sluice down her trunk a moment before washing off.

And when she stepped from the shower and reached for the towel bar, her reflection in the mirror caught her eye and she paused, touching a scar on her belly. Her stomach rolled, but she fought the nausea.

She'd been thrilled with the way Blake had taken her. But of course, you can't make love to a man without getting undressed. At least not forever. Eventually during a round of sex you had to remove your clothes, or at least explain why you wouldn't take off your shirt.

Jax closed her eyes, seeking a sense of calm, but the pounding that suddenly came from the door made achieving a state of Zen impossible.

"Jax," Blake called through the door. "Are you okay? Damn it—" The pounding grew louder, but it was the concern in his voice that pushed her to consider following through on his command. "Open up."

Sucking in a breath, she hastily tossed her pajama top on, ensuring it covered every inch. Her wet skin molded the cloth to her body. As the pounding escalated, she jerked the towel from the bar and wrapped it around her waist.

She opened the door a crack, lifting her chin and meeting Blake's thunderous expression with as much cool as she could muster. Guilt and a self-directed anger were stamped on his face. He took one look at her, swore and began to pace the hallway. Oddly enough, the vision brought a serenity she hadn't thought possible.

Because someone needed to remain calm, and, for the first time, it looked as if Blake Bennington wasn't capable.

And she'd been right. He wore briefs, the fabric stretched tight across a mouthwateringly firm, very taut backside. Her body throbbed with memory, and when he pivoted to pace back, she forced her gaze to his face. This conversation was too important to gawk like a schoolgirl.

Do not look down, Jax. Do not look down.

Shoving a hand through his hair, he stopped short and raked his eyes down her form, as if checking for wounds.

But those were well healed, thank you very much, and had nothing to do with the awkwardness now.

"I'm fine," she said in her most reassuring voice. "I shouldn't have walked away. I'm sure you could have done without all the melodrama. So I apologize." She pushed the door open the rest of the way and leaned against the bathroom doorjamb. No man should have to deal with all of her crazy. "You deserved better."

The height of his eyebrows was almost comical. "What are you talking about?" He threw out his hand, gesturing toward her bedroom door. "For God's sakes. You should have been made love to in a bed."

"I liked our circumstances."

Dark was good. Clothed was *perfect*.

He ignored her response. "If anyone deserved better, it was you."

She crossed her arms. "I was getting exactly what I wanted. Why did we have to stop just when we were getting to the good stuff?" She let out a wistful sigh. "I was having a pretty nice time until you decided to freak out on my behalf."

Blake's eyes went wide. "A nice time?" he said. "You were wincing with the pain." He folded his arm across his bare chest, and Jax forced herself not to ogle the man with the well-muscled torso and iron-hard thighs on display.

He enunciated each word clearly as he said, "And I did not freak out."

"Well, I wasn't wincing with pain," she said. He tipped his head and shot her a you're-lying look. "Okay, I'll admit I was wincing a little with pain," she went on with a resigned sigh, stepping closer as she met his gaze. "But it also felt good."

The pause was heavy, and she knew Blake still wanted her. She could see it in his eyes.

But the overly responsible man couldn't seem to let go of his guilt. "And it could have felt even better if I'd known you weren't kidding about being a virgin," he said. "I would have slowed down." His voice shifted lower. "I'd have chosen a position that might have been a little easier on a first-timer's body."

Ignoring her own throbbing need, she sent him a small smile. "I liked that position," she said, pleased when a flicker of heat reappeared in his eyes.

"It was too much for you," he said softly.

Her heart sounded loud in her ears. "Why don't you let me be the judge of that?"

The four-heartbeat pause lasted forever.

Until he said, "So...what do you want?"

She studiously ignored the masculine cut of his body that had driven her to such a state of distraction that she, for once, had been too caught up in the pleasure to pull away. The sprinkling of dark hair on his chest was the perfect accompaniment to the well-defined abs, tanned skin stretched over the hard plane of chest that tasted as good as it looked.

And, for as long as she lived—no matter *what* came next—she'd relish the memory of Blake coming unglued and driving into her with a passion that was electrifying.

Her need shifted higher. "I want to finish what we started."

The fire in his eyes returned with a vengeance, stealing Jax's breath.

"Okay," he said, his voice rough. "But this time we do this in a bed. And you're on top."

"Every woman's dream, I'm sure," she murmured. "But I was kind of hoping my first time I could just relax and enjoy the ride, so to speak."

He ignored her horrible attempt at humor, clearly oblivious to the fact that she wasn't kidding. His gray eyes radiated an insistence that, this time, she would follow his directions.

"You're on top," he repeated. "That way you control the moment. Keep it more comfortable."

She bit her lower lip, considering her options.

And then his face softened, as if he suddenly clued in to her dilemma. "I can still guide you."

Two heartbeats later, she managed to respond. "Okay," she said. "Count me in."

The desire that flashed through his eyes was fierce, and he reached for the hem of her pajama top. Instinctively, she placed her hand on her shirt, thwarting his attempt.

"But the top stays on," she said.

The pause that followed was long.

She could see the question in his eyes. She'd reveal the complete truth later, but right now she also couldn't risk another round of explanations. A second too-close-to-the-bone discovery would kill the moment for good. And if she didn't get to finish what she'd started with Blake, and soon, she just might die of want.

"The shirt stays on," she repeated in her best matter-of-fact tone.

Eyes dark, he ran a finger up along the curve of her breast, her damp shirt plastered to her skin, and her heart thudded hard.

"Wet shirts are fine by me," he murmured, and then his face grew concerned. "But I have to get a condom from my pants pocket."

"I have a couple on my nightstand." As his brow crinkled in surprise, she said, "I was hoping you'd break the no-kissing rule eventually."

His expression settled into one of pure desire. "Oh..." He tugged the towel from her waist, and it slipped to the floor. "That's one of many rules I'll enjoy breaking."

The mind-melting thrill resurfaced, and he linked his fingers with hers, leading her down the hall and into the bedroom. He shed his briefs and stretched out on the bed, his naked body lit by the light of the moon.

She'd died and gone to heaven for sure.

A touch of nerves returned, but, eyes on Blake, taking

comfort in his gaze, Jax straddled his hips. "Careful, Suit," she said as she ran her hands up his muscular torso, relishing the hard feel. "First it's the no-kissing rule. Next you'll be running red lights at night when no one is looking."

But it was that sense of responsibility that made him perfect for her first time. She knew he was dedicated to making things right again.

Bracing her hands on his chest, she leaned in for a kiss. The lips that fascinated her moved firmly beneath her mouth even as he let her set the pace. But the tongue that rasped against hers spoke of a barely leashed restraint, hinting at the fire to come. He tasted of desire. Of *need*. A sensual mix of moist heat and hard lips. Hands cupping her breasts, he began to rake his thumb across the tips over and over, as if to prime her body, and she moaned, already wet from their aborted first attempt. And growing needlessly wetter from the profound pleasure.

"You don't look confused by your feelings," he murmured against her mouth.

Still engaged with his, her lips quirked at the reminder of her words on the boat. "I'm not."

In response, he raked her nipples harder, making her groan.

Eyes dark, he pulled his mouth away. "But are you outraged by my touch on your chaste skin?"

"Yes, I am," she whispered. His hands working their magic, the heat between her legs grew hotter. Demanding release. "I'm pissed off because you aren't going fast enough."

With a low chuckle, he raised his head and took a nipple in his mouth. The stab of pleasure was fierce, and Jax arched her back, crying out.

He suckled her through the shirt, until she grew desperate, and Jax fumbled for the condom on the bedside table. Blake relieved her of the packet, sheathing himself in latex.

And then he folded his arms behind his head. "This is my first time with a first-timer."

His self-satisfied, almost primal look—combined with the teasing eyes and the disappointing lack of his mouth on her breast—snapped the last of her doubts. She gripped his wrists, pinning them above his head, and the aroused look he shot her made her feel powerful.

"Stop talking." She lowered herself down his hard shaft, and his lids flared with satisfaction even as her body softened, welcoming his return. She shifted her hips, her body readjusting to his, tentatively taking more, and the groan from Blake sent sparks shooting up her spine. Spurring her on. So she rose and lowered herself again, angling her body to take him deeper.

"Jax," he said hoarsely, and she covered his mouth with hers.

Enjoying the rough return of his kiss, the taste of his tongue and his hard shaft inside her, she pressed his hands more firmly to the bed as she began to ride him. The pleasurable pressure drove her insane, and Jax began to roll her hips with determination, relishing the needy, delicious ache between her legs that had been so long in coming.

And so worth the wait.

"Jax," he groaned. "Let go of my hands."

Instead, in answer to his call, she increased the speed of her movements. "Not yet," she whispered, gently nipping his lip.

He hissed and his hips strained beneath hers, the fiery look in his eyes communicating that Blake Bennington was struggling. Fighting hard to keep his reactions in check. She loved that she brought him so close to the edge. She loved that he seemed determined to allow her free rein, encouraging her to take as much as she wanted without the worry of discomfort.

And take she did. Hungry for more, she drew her knees higher, capturing more of his hard shaft, longing to satisfy the terrible ache. Face flushed with heat, her neck damp, she grew desperate, her movements now jerky, almost awkward.

"Jax," he murmured harshly, his eyes intense as he looked up at her. "Let go of my hands."

Too far gone for teasing, she obeyed. Instantly, Blake splayed one hand low on her back, taking over, aiding her movements to receive his hard thrusts. Other hand on her hip, his thumb began to stroke her clitoris.

Pleasure clamped tight around her every nerve ending, holding her hostage and shoving her closer to complete oblivion. She bucked. She writhed. She might have even begged. Until, with one hard stroke of Blake's thumb, it was a done deal. Eyes wide, she dug her nails into his shoulders as the waves of her orgasm swallowed her whole, consumed her, and she collapsed against his chest.

Blake wrapped his arms around her waist and buried his face at her neck, pumping his hips hard, his voice rough as he called out her name and came.

CHAPTER SEVEN

HEART THUMPING HARD, body slick with sweat, Blake held Jax close, his heaving breaths moving against the delicious curves of the pajama-top-covered breasts flattened against his chest. He closed his eyes, slowly coming down from the incredibly intense high, his body relaxing one muscle at a time.

Jax mumbled against his shoulder, "How was your first time with a first-timer?"

A grin captured the corner of his mouth. "Nothing like I expected."

No surprise there. Jax was one of a kind. Unique. A sexy, smart-mouthed woman who was an incomparable mix of sassy confidence, street smarts and beguiling innocence.

Hands on his shoulders, she didn't move anything except her head, lifting her gaze to meet his. "Is that a good thing?" she asked, her eyes narrowing a bit. "Or bad?"

His heart twisted at the vulnerable look, and he tucked a wild strand of tawny hair behind her ear. "You were amazing," he said, his voice low as he ignored the rumbling vibration of need tightening in his groin. He shoved aside the sudden and surprising feeling of possessiveness.

"But I have one question," he said.

"What's that?"

He lifted her arm and kissed the tattoo on her skin. "What

are you going to do with this now? Change the notes to another song?"

Her hazel eyes crinkled in amusement. "Probably tattoo a circle with a line through it over the whole thing."

He chuckled, delighted by the no-holds-barred woman who plunged heart-first into everything she did, and to hell with the consequences.

The thought brought a line of concern in his brow. "Don't forget we have your first court appearance tomorrow."

"I remember," she said with a reluctant groan. "But you promised me a one-night stand, Suit." She slipped her arms around his neck, a heated look returning. "And that means you're mine until the sun comes up."

Desire surged again, and he rolled, sweeping her beneath him as he positioned himself on top.

Her breath hitched softly, and the heat in her voice increased as she shifted her hips beneath him, adjusting to his now fully reformed erection. "No more concessions for the innocent among us?"

"If those were your innocent ways—" he buried his head in her neck, inhaling the scent of strawberry shampoo before shifting until his mouth hovered over hers expectantly "—God help me if you grow bolder."

And the sex that followed only confirmed that Blake was indeed in serious trouble.

The next day Jax leaned back and shifted uncomfortably against the wooden bench in the courthouse hallway. This morning she'd opened her eyes to a rising sun, alone in bed with nothing but her pajama top on, a sheet covering her bare bottom and a note from Blake reminding her of her court appearance.

She puffed out a breath, running a hand down her new black-and-white cotton dress with a gathered tube top, dread tightening in her belly, cutting off any hope of a casual demeanor. A woman's first morning-after should not take place on the day she's scheduled to go before a judge, but Jax had decided that anything worth experiencing was worth experiencing in style.

So far, the decision wasn't making her feel better.

As people streamed by, Jax tried hard not to constantly search for Blake. If he didn't show, she was screwed. If he *did* show, she was screwed. She needed his reassuring presence while standing before a judge. Yet she dreaded having an audience while navigating the awkwardness of their new relationship, courtesy of one incredibly delicious night.

But was the one night all she was going to get?

When Blake turned into the hallway, her body did a double take, his obligatory suit clinging to a hard body that she now knew more intimately than she knew her own. And it was unnerving to realize her lips, teeth and tongue had blazed trails across the tanned skin stretched against hard muscle and sinew. There wasn't a spot she hadn't adored, and there were probably several where she'd left marks. The memory burned, heating her face. And when Blake's gaze finally caught hers, his steps slowing, Jax's heart did a wobbly somersault.

As he came closer, his brow crumpled in surprise. "You're wearing a dress."

And those were *not* the first words she'd expected from of his mouth.

Summoning her patience, she stood and folded her arms across her chest, the feminine black blazer adding a touch of class over her casual dress, the black leggings and funky high heels appealing to her sense of fun. The fact her black-and-white leather platform shoes flirted with a 1930s mobster attitude seemed to fit the occasion.

She hiked a single brow. "After bolting from my bed this morning, is that all you have to say?"

For a brief moment, his mouth grew tight, but before the tension had time to settle, he let out a sigh of resignation. But his low voice didn't detract from the firm tone. "This is neither the time nor the place for this discussion."

"Discussing it over breakfast would have been nice."

He lifted a brow drily. "I had to be at a meeting at seven."

Jax winced. "Okay, so maybe six a.m. was a little early for a discussion." She tipped her head. "But you could have at least woken me up to say goodbye."

His eyebrow hiked a fraction. "I tried," he said, obviously amused. "But you were out cold."

Probably because she'd gone and died from pleasure.

"My exhausted state was as much your fault as mine," she said.

Blake's eyes flashed with an intriguing combination of heat and caution, leaving Jax both aroused and frustrated. Because it was clear from his behavior that he hadn't become her lover; he was simply a man who had spent hours teaching her how much more pleasurable an orgasm was when it involved two people instead of one. To be fair, he had laid out his conditions from the start. And as they studied each other, his expression didn't budge, and she let go of her last bit of hope for more.

"I really am only getting one night, aren't I?" she said.

He shifted on his feet, having the decency to at least look as if he regretted his upcoming words. "Not only do I have your legal battle to contend with, but I'm also in the midst of the biggest case of my career," he said. "So I need to…" He paused, as if determined to get this right. "I need to focus."

She stared at his face, lingering briefly on the lips that not only *looked* sensual, but were also exceptionally skilled at making her cry out, amazed by the variety of embarrassing sounds that could come from her mouth.

"Blake," a male voice said from down the hallway.

Pushing the stimulating thoughts aside, Jax watched the gray-headed man approach. Another Suit with a lawyerly air.

The older man stopped and clapped Blake on the back. "Good to see you, son."

Blake made a quick introduction, and then the two chatted briefly about a case.

And before the man moved on, he leaned in close, as if sharing exciting news. "By all reports the Menendez case is a slam dunk," the man said. "Word has it your name tops the list for promotion to chief of your division. Sounds like a move up the career ladder is in your near future." Jax tried not to let her surprise show as the gentleman went on, his face softening with affection. "Your father would have been proud."

An emotion flickered across Blake's face, too quick for Jax to recognize.

Pride? Determination?

Or was it something else?

"Thank you," Blake said, returning the man's handshake before the gentleman headed off.

Jax turned to Blake, her curiosity now bursting at the seams. "What did your father do?"

He took her elbow and led her down the hallway, and her rebellious heart rejoiced at the return of his touch, even if only for a moment. "He was the U.S. attorney for the southern district of Florida, nominated by the president."

Jax gave a low whistle. "That's an awfully big suit to fill." She frowned slightly. "Are you sure it fits?"

That sensual mouth twitched into an almost smile, but his tone was carefully even. "It fits," he said, obviously sticking with the literal interpretation. He ushered her toward the courtroom door. "I've asked around, and Judge Conner is known for being tough, but fair," he went on, apparently not interested in discussing his father any further.

The familiar smell of his cologne teased her nose, and she was bombarded with images of his naked body, making it difficult to focus.

"This is only an appearance to officially hear the charges

and enter your plea of not guilty," he said. "I'll take care of everything, but if he asks you a direct question, answer it honestly. Otherwise…" He halted just outside the courtroom door, as if rethinking his advice. "Just let me do all the talking." He looked at her with a guarded expression. "Do you think you can handle that?"

She stepped closer, thrilled with the flash of heat in his gaze, and she sent him an overly sweet smile. "Of course I can."

If he thought he could ignore their sizzling chemistry, it was time for *her* to teach him a thing or two. Because she had the advantage of living in his home. And if she spent enough time in her bathing suit by the pool, sooner or later, the man was sure to cave.

At least, that was her plan.…

An hour later Blake escorted Jax back out through the lobby of the courthouse, his hand enjoying the feel of her back and the seductive swing of her unruly, tawny hair against his skin. Her hips swayed in that lissome, loose-limbed way of hers, and his fingers ached to dip lower as he worked diligently to ignore the memories of their night together.

He'd renounced his one-night-stand days long ago, and making Jax an exception to that rule had seemed a reasonable decision. But clearly that had been his libido calling the shots, manipulating his good sense. Given their interactions to date, if he'd been thinking logically he would have realized that *before* he'd slept with her. Being the first to fully taste Jax had certainly never entered his mind as a possibility.

And her unvirgin-like behavior had continued, demanding that he not hold back on any fronts. As if suddenly in a hurry to make up for lost time. And what she'd lacked in experience, she'd more than made up for in enthusiasm, setting his body on fire with her insatiable curiosity.

As the sun had taken its first glimpse over the Atlantic this morning, he'd reluctantly left her bed, spent. Yet invigorated. Still reeling from the night of discovery. Now, six hours later, he still had no idea how to wrap his head around the blistering turn of events.

And his concentration was shot to holy hell.

His gut churned at the disturbing emotions, because he wanted her again, but he willed himself to think logically. To remain rational. Because, despite their night together, he still had a job to do and Jax's legal problem to address. It hadn't been his choice to be in charge of her case, but he'd made a promise and he intended to see it through. Which meant he needed to clarify a few things with the woman. Most notably, that her devil-may-care attitude and smart mouth might prove her undoing.

Because, if ever there was proof that Jacqueline Lee lived by her own rules, today had to be it.

"Just for the record," Blake said with a droll tone, "since it was the judge that brought up the picture of the Ramones on your dress..." He opened the glass door of the lobby and ushered her into the warm sunshine. How could he have missed the full, standing image of the punk-rock band beneath the blazer? "It was perfectly acceptable to acknowledge your agreement with his comment about their impact on rock and roll." The door closed behind them, and he shot Jax a meaningful look. "But engaging in a debate about which band had the most impact on punk rock was not the wisest course of action."

Jax gazed up at him as if she had no idea why the disagreement was a problem. "Judge Conner asked for my opinion and I gave it to him."

He fought the urge to let out an impatient sigh, clearing his throat instead, and shot her the most level look he could manage. "I believe his comment was meant to be a rhetorical question."

Jax simply shrugged. "Well, if he didn't want to hear my

views, then he shouldn't have formed it in the phrase of a question at all."

As they descended the courthouse steps, Blake took a moment to regain his composure before addressing her again.

Narrowing his eyes in mock confusion, he said, "Do you get up every morning looking for ways to make life harder on yourself? Or does that just come naturally?"

Her lips quirked as she slipped off her blazer, draping it over her arm and baring the most beautiful expanse of shoulders Blake had ever had the pleasure of viewing. Desire fisted in his gut, but he ignored the feeling.

"Is this another one of those rhetorical questions that I'm not supposed to answer?" she said lightly.

"Yes," he said, his tone firm. "Absolutely."

She shot him a look from the corner of her eye, tossing back the wild hair that the breeze had plastered to her cheek. Her sweetly innocent smiles, like the one she was sending him now, were not to be trusted.

"You told me to be honest," she said.

Blake bit back a smile at the courtroom memory, refusing to let her see his amusement. "Well, Judge Conner appeared to be enjoying the sixty seconds that it took for you to lay out your arguments in favor of the Ramones, even though he ultimately disagreed with your assessment."

She came to a halt, grinning up at him and sending a disturbing thrill of pleasure along his veins. And the need to keep her out of further trouble made his expression turn serious again.

"You asked me to represent you in court," he said. "In future, I need you to think about your actions and their consequences." He focused on *not* looking down at her sun-kissed skin above the Ramones sundress.

The frown on her face lacked any real heat. "Is this your way of telling me to keep my fat mouth shut?"

He pursed his lips, trying to come up with a diplomatic

response. "It's my way of telling you that the world doesn't need to know your every thought." Against his will, his eyes drifted down to the bared shoulders. "Where did you find that dress, anyway?"

She grinned. "Your mother found it online and gave it to me as a good-luck gift."

Blake suppressed the sigh. "Did she give you the mobster heels, too?" Blake said wryly.

"Nope, that was Nikki." Her eyes lit with humor. "I plan on wearing them to the trial."

Instead of groaning, Blake swiped a hand down his face. Ten years of being the sole responsible Bennington adult had trained him how to remain calm in a crisis, how to retain his cool when either Nikki or his mother had gotten into trouble, as they invariably did.

Now he had Jacqueline Lee to contend with as well, and she was more than a match.

Because this was the woman who'd slayed him with her confident air, charmed him with her endearing vulnerability and brought him to his sexual knees. The only way he was going to be able to keep his hands to himself was if he avoided her altogether.

And he hoped that wouldn't be harder than he thought.

Two weeks later, Jax leaned against the center island in Blake's kitchen, rechecking the spreadsheet on her laptop. The phone fundraiser for the club had ended, and, as she entered the last bit of data, the results were looking *abysmal*. So, it would seem, did her chances of ever touching Blake again.

How could she have thought living in his house would be an advantage?

Nikki balanced her crutches under her arms. "Have a tally yet?"

Jax struggled to push the thoughts of Blake aside. "Nope."

At Nikki's concerned face, a wave of gratitude hit. "No matter what happens," she said, "thanks for helping."

"Are you kidding?" Nikki hobbled to the counter. "Boy, you have no idea how glad I am you're here," the pretty brunette stated with feeling, her clear gray eyes so like her brother's that it was impossible *not* to think of Blake. Nikki reached across the marble counter for one of her mother's peppermint scones. "Despite the fact that he never misses a chance to remind me of my most recent screwup, at least he's usually good for a laugh. But lately my uptight big brother has been avoiding me more than usual," she said and then nibbled on her scone with a furrow of concern between her eyebrows.

Jax wasn't sure if the concern was in response to the taste of the scone or her worries about Blake.

And, with every mention of the man, Jax struggled with the heat that threatened to overtake her cheeks. Since it was hopeless, she dipped her head, letting her hair curtain her face as she pretended to check the dismal fundraiser total to date. Steering the discussion away from Nikki's brother was critical. Blake had already taken over her dreams... commandeered her every fantasy. No sense in suffering his virtual presence during the daytime, as well.

Of course, after two weeks of living on pins and needles and various other sharp objects, hoping for a glimpse of the Suit who dominated her thoughts, she'd finally resigned herself to the fact that her previous plan was hopeless.

Seducing an absent man was impossible.

Jax entered a few more figures into her laptop. "I doubt he's avoiding you, Nikki. It's probably just your imagination," she said in an even tone, hoping that would be the end of Blake as the topic of conversation.

"I don't think so," Nikki said, her eyes hinting at the misery beneath, and Jax's heart twisted in sympathy. "Even though his case is at the crazy stage, he used to at least try to make it home for dinner. These days, unless you're up at the crack of dawn to see him walk out the door, you wouldn't even know he lived here."

"I'm sure it's not a reflection on you."

More of a reflection on my presence.

Nikki tossed her leftover scone onto her plate. "No. He's still angry at me over the whole zip-line incident," she said with a roll of her eyes. "You should have seen his expression when he showed up at the hospital."

Nikki pulled a face and propped her elbows on the counter, chin on her hands, and Jax's compassion for the siblings swelled, their relationship more deeply troubled than she'd originally thought. At the hospital Blake had probably hid his fear behind his fury. And Nikki, no doubt, had gone all snarky in defense. Despite hoping for a change in topic, Jax felt obligated to point out the obvious.

"But he came for you," Jax said softly.

A shadow flitted across Nikki's face. "Yeah," she said slowly, turning her gaze to the window and the shimmering pool beyond, looking almost...lost. "Mom was off on a month-long cruise with her cronies. Unavailable, as usual." Her voice then shifted lower, almost self-critical. "With me being the typical pain in Blake's ass."

Guilt roiled in Jax's gut, because she knew Blake's absenteeism had more to do with her than his sister. "As a matter of fact, I'm pretty sure the pain-in-Blake's-ass title is reserved for me."

"How so?" Nikki asked, and Jax froze.

Nice way to steer the conversation in uncomfortable directions, Jax.

She cleared her throat. "Oh, you know," Jax said with a vague tone as she concentrated on entering the last set of figures into the computer. "He was never thrilled about handling my case."

The final tally popped on-screen, and Jax let out a groan. Glad for the change in topic, but sorry about the news, she pivoted her computer to show Nikki, her lips twisting wryly. "Have any other friends who need help with a broken leg?" Jax said, trying to sound light when her heart was heavy.

Nikki looked at the number and winced. "Don't give up hope yet," she said. "We'll figure something out."

Staring at the computer as if searching for the answer, the brunette nibbled cautiously on a peanut-butter muffin. After confirming it was edible, she took a tentative bite before making a face of regret. Jax leaned a hip against the counter, trying hard not to feel regret herself.

Regretting the loss of her job and missing out on more with Blake.

She wanted Blake's hungry hands on her body again. She needed his mouth on her skin, trailing those hot kisses that liquefied her bones and made her weep. More important, she longed for the kind of completion that involved a give-and-take, the shared pleasure an ecstasy of the acutest kind. And the longer she went without, the clearer it became that she'd never be satisfied with solitary activities ever again.

Abigail Bennington breezed into the kitchen. "Goodness, girls," Blake's mother said. "What's with all the negative vibes?"

I lost my virginity to your son yet all he'll give me is one night.

Fortunately, Nikki answered for her instead. "Jax is having trouble raising money for her music program at the club."

Jax tried to push Blake from her mind. "The current economic environment is tight," she said, feeling defeated. "Too much need and not enough dollars to go around."

Abigail pulled up a bar stool at the center island and took a seat. "That's simple," she said, running her fingers through her short salt-and-pepper hair. "What you need, Jax, is a media-worthy event."

"I tried that," Jax said doubtfully. "It didn't work."

"Something big enough to *really* get the public's attention," Blake's mother said. "And I just happen to be an expert."

"An expert in what?" Jax asked.

"Creating a scene," Abigail said proudly. And then she leaned forward, the excitement oozing from her lined face. "So listen, chickadees. This is what we're going to do...."

Several days later, Blake ignored the protesters chanting on the flat-screen TV and inhaled the scent of freshly baked bread, maneuvering through the lunchtime crowd of the delicatessen just across from his office. Many of the diners were from his division. Several called out to him as he passed, wishing him luck with the case or telling him it was in the bag.

Blake wished he felt so confident. The closing arguments were set to start soon, and he knew the proceedings were going well for him. But one thing he'd learned through the years, no matter how open-and-shut the case, one could never be absolutely sure until the verdict was returned. Because human beings were unpredictable. Put twelve jurors together in a room, people with hopes and dreams and varying experiences, and anything could happen.

Jax was a prime example. She was one of the most unpredictable women he'd ever met, which had the unfortunate effect of making her the most exciting woman he'd ever slept with.

The sensual memory slid down his spine, spreading low in his gut.

Blake wasn't quite sure how he felt about the turn of events. Fortunately his case was revving up for the final days, consuming his every waking moment. Except there were a lot of moments when his mind would drift off, delicious images of Jax tripping up his focus. And what good did it do to avoid the pretty little distraction if his mind was consumed with thoughts of her anyway?

He was beginning to think he'd be better off with her in his bed every night. At least then he wouldn't be constantly questioning his one-night-only rule.

Brow bunched in doubt, Blake paid for his sandwich and headed for a table. When the pretty, blond attorney from the civil division sent him a tentative smile, a welcoming look in her eye, and he felt absolutely no inclination to even chat with her, he knew he was in more trouble than he'd thought.

Because the sleek, polished beauty paled in comparison to the wild, reckless charm of Jax.

Blake carried his sandwich past the blonde's table, pretending he was interested in one of several TV monitors blasting the midday news. But he didn't care about the current footage of a chanting, discontented crowd, too distracted by the possibility of renegotiating his initial plan. Maybe he *could* do his job and still spend a little time with Jax? Maybe he would be more efficient if he wasn't constantly wondering when he'd see the little hellion on heels again? And he was perfectly capable of—

"Hey, Blake," one of the boys from the narcotics division called out. "Isn't that your sister on the TV?"

Heart plummeting like a dropped concrete block, Blake shifted his eyes back to one of the flat-screens.

And there, in the middle of a well-attended protest—under the watchful eye of a line of *police*—stood his sister holding a poster, her arms resting on her crutches. The dragon on her cast now elaborately breathed out a whoosh of fire that extended to her toes.

And standing beside Nikki, mouth clearly cheering along with the crowd, was Jax.

Blake's jaw clenched and his grip on his sandwich grew tight, sending blobs of chicken salad plopping to his plate. His heart picked up speed as he stood, his chair scraping loudly against the tile, and tried to decide who he was going to kill first.

Nikki...or Jax?

CHAPTER EIGHT

JAX HAD BEEN SUMMONED to appear before a judge before and had handled that with a bit of composure, so why was she letting her upcoming meeting with Blake get to her? Regardless, her heart picked up speed as she drew nearer to his home office. Hoping for the best.

Expecting the worst.

They had just been winding up their day at the protest when Blake had shown up, his disapproving expression hard, his grim, lawyerly attitude firmly in place. He'd said little as he'd calmly, coolly, but with the deadliest voice imaginable, informed them that it was time to go home. Not wishing to tire out Nikki, Jax had been ready to take his sister back to the house anyway. But based on the general principles of freedom and democracy—and all those other truly elusive ideals—Jax had considered telling him no. Something in his gaze made her, for once, hold her tongue.

His gray eyes had resembled the color of steel, the memory distracting as she'd come home and assisted Nikki with her technically challenging daily bath, helping to shampoo the morning's road dust from the brunette's hair. As she'd settled Nikki by the pool with her ereader, Blake had passed by, shooting Jax a curt "Meet me in my office when you're done," his tone sending anxious ants crawling up her spine. Nikki's whispered words—"I'll give you an hour and then come search for your dead body"—had hardly helped Jax's confidence, either.

So Jax had returned to her guesthouse for a quick shower and change of clothes. Because no way was she going to go toe-to-toe with power-suit-wearing Blake while sporting a T-shirt sticky with dried sweat and reeking of car fumes.

Needing the courage of a good butt-kicking country tune, but knowing a soundtrack wasn't an option for the upcoming scene with Blake, she'd pulled on her cowboy boots instead. Now, in clean cutoffs, every step brought Jax closer to Blake's office, making her heart thump harder as her heels clomped down the hallway. She took comfort in her cotton T-shirt with the reassuring image of the original queen of the divas, Aretha Franklin. When she reached the doorway, she paused to take in the room. The Italian tile was a soothing mocha color, and that, combined with the hunter-green walls and rich leather furniture, created a very masculine atmosphere. Pristine and immaculate and oh-so-Blake.

And Jax was growing tired of waiting for the man to decide he wanted her again.

Blake stood at the window, his back to her, watching Nikki, who had fallen asleep on her chaise longue under the patio umbrella. But he must have heard Jax's approach.

Without turning to face her, his voice low, he said, "What the hell were you thinking?"

Her nerves stretched tighter even as irritation surged at his tone, and she fisted her hand at her side, resolving to remain calm.

No matter how annoying the man became.

"I was thinking I had a problem to solve," Jax said.

"Solve it how?" He turned to face her, his expression carved from stone. "By risking another arrest?"

"Everything was legit. We followed the letter of the law," Jax said. "Nikki and I obtained the protest permit. And your mother—"

"My mother?" he said, and, from the tone of his voice, Jax was amazed his eyes didn't pop from his head. "You dragged my mother into your fight?"

Jax fought for patience. "I didn't drag her. She volunteered," Jax said, and then her expression softened with affection. Growing up, she'd wondered what her own mother had been like. She'd always pictured someone as kind and supportive as Abigail. Though preferably a better cook...

"It was her idea," Jax went on. "And she's been really helpful—"

"Helpful," Blake repeated with a scoffing sound.

Jax's patience slipped a bit and she entered his office, coming to a stop beside his massive desk. She planted her fisted hand on her hip. "This discussion is going to take a long time if you keep interrupting me."

"I'll do you one better," Blake said, sarcasm oozing from his tone as he started to pace. "Because my day was interrupted when I got a glimpse of a news clip of my sister, the one who is studying to become a lawyer—and the woman I'm trying to help beat a charge of disturbing the peace—at a freakin' protest surrounded by the *police*."

He came to a stop in front of her, his proximity imposing. "Do you know how difficult it would be to defend you against the first set of charges if you had a second set pending?"

She inhaled a steadying breath, knowing her composure was wearing thin. "I told you, we did everything according to the law," she said. "We had no intention of doing anything that would cause trouble."

A second bark of skepticism burst from his mouth. "Just like you didn't plan on getting arrested during your performance at a flash mob?"

She bit her cheek, counting out her thudding heartbeats until she was calm enough to respond. "Yes," she said, her lips tight. "It's amazing I've managed to make it to twenty-three years of age without your help."

And while her anger was taking on a life of its own, a part of her—a little bitty part—was pleased that he was mad. Perhaps, subconsciously, she'd agreed to Abigail's suggestion of a protest in hopes it *would* piss him off. She was tired of his logic and reason. She was tired that she was the only one in this relationship that seemed to be affected. But mostly, she was tired of wondering when he was going to *want* her again.

Maybe she hadn't had much experience. Quite frankly, she didn't care that he had been her first. Damn it, she knew the sex had been good. Spectacular, even. So how could he continue to stay away?

Outside of their single night together, she'd never know by his behavior that they'd slept together. The man was entirely too composed.

So let him be angry.

"If you're so hell-bent on being convicted of a misdemeanor and permanently losing your job," he said, "feel free."

The judgmental tone strained her last, and very tenuous, strand of patience.

"That's right," she said, the words tight as she stepped closer. "I do feel free." She hadn't bounced from home to home as a kid only to continue to be at the mercy of the world around her. Mr. Uptight had another think coming if he thought she scared that easily. "It's *my* choice. *My* decision. *My life*."

Blake watched Jax's chest heave with barely controlled fury, his head thumping, his anger a living entity in his head.

The heavy weight of responsibility threatened to crush him. He was tired of being the one to clean up everyone else's mess. Of being the only one to think of the consequences. For once he'd like to live the fun and carefree life of his college years, the kind Nikki and his mother and Jax seemed to be enjoying every day.

And why had everyone else's good sense died and left him in charge?

The thought of Nikki ruining her future, carelessly limiting her career before it had even begun, still burned in Blake's gut. Learning to live with his role in his father's death had almost crippled him, and he hated the thought of Nikki permanently paying for a momentary lapse in judgment. He'd promised his father he'd take care of his sister, and he damn well was going to follow through. And that meant helping her steer clear of the kind of regrets that caged your soul.

But Jax wasn't family, so why was he just as disturbed by her choices?

Fear made his words hard. "If you want to sabotage your career, that's your business," he said, fighting to ignore Jax's freshly scrubbed beauty, the lightly tanned legs bared beneath a pair of libido-disturbing cutoffs. And those sexy cowboy boots.

Man, was it the woman's purpose in life to drive him insane?

"But I will not allow you to ruin my sister's future as a lawyer by dragging her into your fight."

A flash of concern flickered through her eyes, and he knew the emotion was real. He'd watched them together; he'd seen the growing affection. Jacqueline Lee might not care if she risked her own future, but he knew she cared about his sister's.

Which was what made her actions doubly frustrating.

Her mouth twitched with self-doubt. "I would never do anything to hurt Nikki."

He stared at her beautifully flushed face, refusing to look away. Anything to keep his gaze from those seductive legs and the disturbing memories of them wrapped around his waist. "Then leave her out of your fight."

Her voice was harsh. "Fine."

As their gazes continued to clash, he tensed and his jaw

hardened, dismayed that he found little satisfaction in her agreement. Dismayed that he cared that Jax was intent on taking foolish risks.

Dismayed that he cared...

He took a step closer to Jax, unable to prevent himself from going on. "And stop jeopardizing your case by continuing to create a public stir," he said. "You need to quit with the I'm-a-free-spirit attitude and *start* thinking about how your actions will be viewed by others."

The look that flashed through her eyes made it clear he'd chosen his argument poorly. Damn the fickle nature of human emotion. The woman should come with a warning label. The already heavy air pressed in around him as the moments ticked by and he waited for Jax to choose her defense.

"My actions are none of your business," she said.

"You made them my business."

"Fine," she huffed. "Then I don't want your help anymore."

"You *need* my help," he boomed. "I just want you to stop threatening your case by going out of your way to be such a bloody nonconformist."

The pause that followed was thick.

Until she held up her wrist, displaying the two linear marks decorated with ink. "Do you see these scars?" she said, and his chest grew tight, sensing bad news was coming.

"As a teen I carved them because it was better to feel the pain physically than to bear it in my heart," she said.

The words struck him hard, burning through his gut. His heart thundering, he opened his mouth to offer words of comfort, but she held up her hand to stop him.

Their gazes locked, his breath froze, his throat tight.

"You want me to change?" A few moments later she dropped her arm to her side, her eyes still flashing, her gaze inches from his. "Well, too bad. Because I spent years being shuffled from foster home to foster home. Depressed that others thought I wasn't good enough to fit with their family.

After a while it was impossible not to believe that there was something really wrong with *me*."

She hiked her chin proudly. "But I don't buy into that self-esteem-destroying crap anymore. Because with the help of the teen club and an incredibly kindhearted volunteer—" she placed a hand on the image of Aretha Franklin plastered across her breasts "—I learned that I am a beautiful, intelligent woman who deserves respect. And I do not need *you*—" she jabbed a finger at his chest "—to tell me how to live my life."

"Jax—"

"And I *refuse* to let fear or self-doubt rule my future," she said, and then she stepped back and jerked her shirt to just beneath her breasts, revealing an abdomen completely covered in a crisscrossing linear pattern of purplish scars.

A body blow of epic proportions hit Blake, draining the blood from his face, leaving him dizzy.

Eyes snapping, she said, "Because I've been there before and I'm not going back."

An ugly swearword burst from his mouth, and he fought for control as he took in the sight of months'—perhaps *years'*—worth of scars. Not an inch was left unmarked, her skin disfigured from the self-mutilation. Grief and horror and tenderness gripped him so tight his eyes stung with the emotion.

"Jesus, Jax," he croaked, stepping closer, his stomach threatening to reject what little of his sandwich he'd consumed.

She met his eyes, chin still high, her expression stoic. "Don't feel sorry for me," she said, her voice hard. "I don't want or need your sympathy. I am proud of who I am and how I live my life." Confidence and passion and conviction radiated from her face as she enunciated each word clearly, her gaze boring into his as she went on. "Because I'm a goddamn warrior who has earned her stripes."

His chest heaving, a host of emotions battled for supremacy. Fierce admiration. A profound humility. And a sliver of jealousy that this woman, a woman who had lived through hell and come back fighting, had attained what was slipping further and further from his grasp every day. Living life on her own terms instead of denying what she wanted in deference to logic.

Duty versus need.

Lust versus reason.

Making love to Jax or continuing to deny himself.

He sucked in a breath, and, against his will, his gaze drifted to the pink lips that were set in a determined line.

Eyes dark, she lowered her shirt as she stepped close enough to bring the scent of lavender back. Her passion, her strength and her beauty—both inside and out—tightened its grip around his spine.

"And unless you plan on touching me again, Suit," she said in a low voice, "stop looking at me like you don't know whether to make love to me or scold me like a rebellious kid."

His heart pounded as if attempting to free its way from his chest, and a little of his resolve cracked, providing just enough room for the climbing pressure to gain a foothold. And the man who took what he wanted without thought of the consequences—the wild rebel he'd been suppressing for *years*—escaped in a rush.

With an explicit curse, Blake hooked his hand behind the hellion on heels' neck and pulled, her body colliding with his, his mouth landing hard on her lips.

With a sigh, Jax melted against Blake's unyielding chest, returning the rough, raw kiss with all the fire and longing that had been building for weeks. After an incredible night with Blake, followed by many a restless sleep, it was a relief to be back in his arms. Not just because of the need to be free to touch him again or the need to feel the relatively new, and blissfully wonderful, experience of full-on sex again. The most profound relief came from Blake finally knowing the true extent of her past.

And wanting her anyway.

No I-can't-escape-your-presence-fast-enough expression like Jack. No horrified gleam in his eyes that communicated she'd launched beyond cute-crazy and straight into scary-crazy. Instead, Blake's mouth was taking hers in a blatant sign of possession, as if acknowledging it all and verifying he didn't care. His lips slanted across hers hungrily, his tongue impatient against hers. It was an act of control. A stamp of ownership.

Who knew a little domination would be such a turn-on?

Lips controlling hers, his movement tinged with an angry desperation, Blake shrugged out of his coat, his jacket hitting the floor as he gave his tie an impatient jerk. "Lock the door," he ordered against her mouth.

In the time it took Jax to comply, Blake had his shirt and shoes off. Eyes on his gloriously heart-stopping erection beneath his pants, her throat suddenly dry, she crossed back to his desk.

Gaze dark with need, he hooked his finger in her waistband and yanked her closer, unsnapping her shorts and pushing the cutoffs to the floor. "I have to be back at the office by three."

With an overwhelming sense of freedom, she peeled off her shirt, baring her abdomen in all its horrific glory, and tossed Aretha aside. "I have plans for cocktails and a lecture on subversive protesting technique with your mother at four."

With a frown, he took her lips in another mind-melting, do-as-I-say, openmouthed kiss that communicated that, this time, he was calling all the shots.

This was the bossy side she could never get enough of....

He pulled back, his eyes made of steel. "No subversive protests."

"Okay," she said, shucking her panties with a shimmy of

her hips, stepping out of the lace and kicking it aside. "I'll just humor her and pretend to take notes."

He cupped her breasts together and brought his mouth down, impatiently consuming her nipples with his mouth, teeth and tongue. Darts of desire skimmed along her veins, and she arched helplessly against him.

Need made her mind spin as she skimmed her hands across the well-defined muscles in his arms and his deliciously cut chest. She unfastened his pants, pushing them and his briefs to the floor. "As far as Nikki is concerned—" she was already panting in anticipation when she made the mistake of dropping her gaze, and the next thing she knew she was staring at his erection "—we have about an hour."

Which, with the way her body was throbbing, felt wholly inadequate.

He gripped her hips and hauled her against his hot, naked and very aroused shaft, and her body nearly belted out a tune. "How do you figure that?" he said.

"'Cuz that's how long she said she'd wait before coming to look for my dead body," she said as she tipped her right toe against her left heel, ready to slip off a boot.

"Wait," he ordered, and panic paralyzed her.

Her heart racing, fear sluiced through Jax even as her veins hummed with pleasure at his hard length, ramping up her pulse to astronomical rates. Fear that he'd suddenly come to his senses and remember she wasn't the kind of woman he wanted in his life. Worried the reminder of her actions today had thoroughly doused his desire. Terrified that the visible evidence of her turbulent mind-set of long ago was too much for him to deal with.

And God help her, she was desperate to have him take her body.

Gaze burning into hers, voice gruff, he said, "I'm going to make love to you while you wear nothing but those cowboy boots."

Relief swamped her, and she exhaled in a rush. "Jeez, Blake," she said, twining her arms around his neck, "I thought you were going to say you just remembered you had an appointment and needed to leave."

His voice harsh, he said, "Absolutely not."

And the searing kiss that followed sent her senses skyrocketing

He trailed hot kisses across her cheek and down her neck, scraping his teeth across her pulse as he gripped her butt and hauled her up onto his desk. The cool wood couldn't overcome the heat between her legs, and she shifted impatiently as Blake retrieved his wallet from the desk, pulling out a condom.

"Right now..." Eyes burning, he sheathed himself in latex. "There's nothing I need more than you."

The words were the sweetest she'd ever heard. "Does this mean I can permanently disregard the no-kissing clause?" she said, feigning innocence.

He tugged on her knees, positioning her thighs for his body. "I'm burning the damn contract," he muttered darkly, and then he took her with a commanding thrust.

CHAPTER NINE

"So what did my big brother have to say to you in his office earlier today?" Nikki said as she spooned glazed vegetables onto her plate. Blake sat at the head of the dining room table, and Nikki shot him a surreptitious look. "Did he give you his lecture on consequences, like he did me?" Nikki said drily. "Or did he simply tell you that you were ruining your life?"

Across the table from Nikki, Jax shifted in her seat, uncomfortable with Nikki's tone and topic of conversation. Somehow she didn't think Blake's "I'm going to make love to you while you wear nothing but those cowboy boots" was an appropriate response. Though God knew Jax had loved every second of being so thoroughly dominated, the life-changing moment completely minus the kid gloves he'd used their first night together.

A truly liberating experience.

But now was not the time to dwell on the delightful memories, especially with Nikki spoiling for a fight while Blake and Abigail sat at either end of the big dining-room table. Because everyone was waiting for her answer, all eyes currently assessing Jax, Nikki's expectant, Abigail's unconcerned and Blake's...

Well, Blake, damn him. He had the audacity to look amused.

All Jax wanted was to get through her dinner in relative peace.

"Don't start holding back now, Jax," Blake said smoothly. The light in his eyes left her with an overwhelming urge to stick her tongue out at him. "I'd love to hear your version."

She shot him a look she hoped went unnoticed by his family. "Shall I mention the thumbscrews?" she said, her tone falsely light.

Blake's eyes crinkled in the corners. "By all means. And don't forget the rack, either."

The rack brought to mind Blake pinning her to his desk....

Jax forced herself to focus.

"Let me guess," Nikki went on as if to save Jax the trouble. "He dusted off the old you're-going-to-regret-this-later phrase and then gave you a condescending pat on the head with an authoritative air."

Jax's heart sank a little lower, and she wondered why Nikki seemed intent on the conversation now. She'd had all afternoon to discuss the meeting with Jax. In truth, there was only one conclusion: while raking her brother over the coals, Nikki preferred an audience.

Probably in an attempt to give Blake's never-let-'em-see-you-ruffled style a real workout.

At first she'd viewed Blake solely from Nikki's point of view, feeling defensive on the kindred spirit's behalf. But, despite her growing affection for the fun-loving brunette, Jax was fast learning that Nikki never missed an opportunity to goad her brother.

And Jax suspected Nikki provoked Blake just to see him raise that cool, authoritarian head in response.

The relationship ruts these two had dug appeared too deep to ever allow escape to a better way.

"So how did the conversation go?" Nikki said.

Jax bit the corner of her lip, looking to soothe the waters. "After a little bit of a debate—" a debate involving who was the one who got to be on top the next time they made love on his desk "—we…" Jax cleared her throat. "We reached an agreement."

No need to clarify that their accord involved whose bed they'd make love in tonight. And the sense of freedom to enjoy the man's sexy company, without worrying about her past, was heavenly.

"I'm surprised. My brother doesn't usually reach agreements," Nikki said with an edge of resentment. "Mostly he just dispenses judgment and hands out sentences."

There was a slight pause, as if Nikki knew she'd gone too far.

"Nikki, regardless of how you feel about me—" Blake's tone was carefully even "—Jax is a guest in our home. And she deserves a tranquil dinnertime atmosphere."

A frown appeared on Nikki's face as she shot Jax an apologetic look. "I'm sorry you got dragged into our dysfunctional relationship."

Blake's mother finally entered into the conversation. "Ridiculous, Nikki," Abigail said, gleefully untroubled by the tension. "The dysfunctional family is just part and parcel of the American dream. You know, like baseball, apple pie and polarizing politics." The lines bracketing her eyes shifted with triumph. "And, Jax, I forgot to tell you earlier. I contacted my friend Franklin about our funding problem."

At the words *our problem*, a phrase that made her feel less alone, Jax's heart melted a touch. The natural way the family was including her was growing harder to resist. Even the siblings squabbling felt surprisingly…homey.

Jax fought the urge to melt into complete mush as she looked around the table at Blake, his sister and the endearingly eccentric Abigail.

"We might not have accomplished everything I'd wanted with the protest," Blake's mother said as she patted Jax's hand, and Jax steeled herself against the surge of heartwarming emotion. "But we are not a one-trick-pony show. I am

woman, hear me roar, and all that jazz," she said as she carelessly waved her fork in the air. "I have several more ideas
up my sleeves."

"Yeah," Nikki agreed, her face reflecting her excitement.
"I think Mom's idea to find a celebrity endorsement is inspired."

Jax fought the emotional tightening of her throat as she
studied the faces of the two women who'd so eagerly embraced her cause, all in the name of helping her out. Just like
family was supposed to do.

Don't you dare get too attached, Jax.

This wasn't her family, and there was no sense in setting
herself up for disappointment. But it was nice to once, just
once, feel as if she belonged to a unit outside of the club.

With great effort, Jax finally tuned back into Abigail's
speech.

"…because sex sells," Abigail was saying, and Jax studiously ignored the heated look that Blake sent her.

It was painfully obvious he was thinking about their round
of lovemaking today. Jax sent him a shut-up stare. Where was
the coolly controlled man when she needed him? The one that
calmly set her back after her kiss. The one who'd eaten lunch
with them without betraying a hint of attraction? Apparently
Blake was beginning to live life a little more on the edge.

And who was ruining the tranquil dinnertime atmosphere
now?

"So my friend Franklin is going to use his contacts in the
local music industry," Abigail droned on, and Jax struggled
to catch up with the topic. "To see if he can land that sexy
Bulldog as a spokesman for the club."

Blake finally turned his disturbing gaze to his mother in
confusion. "Bulldog?"

"He's the local hip-hop artist that hit the big time." Abigail
shook her head at her son, as if he was derelict in his duties
for not being familiar with the hometown rap star. "He's just

back from a fabulously successful world tour. And," Abigail continued, her grin growing bigger, "he has a body that just screams sex."

Jax got the impression that Blake was striving to ignore his mother's comment, but his reluctance to participate was brought up short when his mother turned to Blake.

"What say you, Blake?" Abigail said.

"I have no idea who the man is, nor am I familiar with his body to die for." A furrow appeared between his brows as he sent his mother a small frown. "And I'm hoping my knowledge of the man's physique continues to be of the nonexistent kind," he added drily. His forehead crinkled in concern. "If he is that well-known, surely he won't have time to take on a club for teens."

"Are you doubting my skills?" Abigail said.

Blake was obviously fighting back a smile as he answered. "I think the man doesn't stand a chance against the powerful female force in this room."

But there was no chastising tone, only acceptance. And a tint of pride.

Nikki pretended to choke on her iced tea. "Did you just pay us a compliment?"

"Blake's being remarkably good-humored tonight," Abigail said. She narrowed her eyes at her only son. "Come to think of it, you look more relaxed than you have in ages, despite the trial that could ruin your career if you fail."

Without missing a beat, Blake lifted a brow. "Thanks for the encouraging words," he said with a wry twist of his lips.

"I'm only trying to be realistic," Abigail said airily. And then a line of curiosity formed between her eyebrows. "Which is usually your job. Yet you seem unusually optimistic." She set her fork down, the lines in her forehead growing deeper. "Why is that?"

Jax felt the inquiry all the way to her curling toes, and silently prayed for tranquility.

Blake shifted in his seat. "The Menendez case goes to jury this week."

"That's not the point," Abigail said. She looked unconcerned about the case. "I don't think it's the end of the trial that has you looking so relaxed."

There was a pause that felt like forever as every blood cell in Jax's face felt as if it expanded twofold.

Nikki lightly thumped her hand on the table. "I knew it," she said, her eyes bright with mischief as she addressed her brother. "You hooked up with that uptight defense attorney, didn't you? The one who's helping you with Jax's case." While Jax blinked back a surge of ridiculous jealousy, Nikki turned to her mother. "I think Blake's dry spell has finally come to an end. And thank God, too," she said, lifting a brow at her brother. "Maybe getting started on those two and half children with the perfect lawyer will get you off my case about my lack of a summer internship. I might just send the lady a thank-you note."

Blake was clearly avoiding Jax's gaze. And the wave of heat that had already crept up her neck now spread across her face. Jax dropped her eyes to her plate of food, pushing her fork through her mashed potatoes as nonchalantly as she could.

Nikki was too busy poking fun at her brother to notice. But, as their mother's gaze shifted from her son to Jax, the comprehension in Abigail's expression was impossible to miss. Jax's heart sank at the perceptive look. Because now his curious mother would probably be showing up more frequently than usual. Bringing more baked goods with her, too.

Jax forced back the sigh as she slumped in her seat. Being under Abigail's sharply amused, watchful eye as she and Blake worked their way through this tentative relationship made things uncomfortable enough.

Suffering through it with an endless succession of weird pastries was asking too much.

* * *

One week and several delicious nights later, the pop of the champagne bottle was loud. His mom let out a celebratory woo-hoo that was even louder. But Blake wasn't sure if his mother's excitement was more of a reflection of his momentous day and the guilty verdict he'd won in the trial, or in anticipation of partaking of the pricey bubbly.

He was fairly certain it was in equal measure of both.

But after two years of dedicating his life to the case, Blake couldn't pin down exactly how he felt. Wrestling with the churning emotions, Blake gripped his glass as his mother filled his champagne flute, followed by Jax's, Nikki's and then her own.

His mother lifted her glass. "A toast to my son's accomplishments."

Jax was looking especially beautiful in her Carrie Underwood T-shirt and jeans that did heart-stopping things to her figure. She murmured a "Hear! Hear!" while Nikki shot him a teasing look.

"Your résumé is getting pretty impressive, big brother," Nikki said.

And it had the potential to get even more impressive, although he hadn't shared that bit of news with his family yet. But if he didn't tell them soon, they'd hear it from someone else.

Inhaling a deep breath, Blake took the plunge. "I was offered the promotion to chief of my division today."

There was a moment of stunned silence, and then his mother set the bottle and her glass down before enveloping him in a huge hug.

"That's fantastic, Blake," she said. She pulled back to look up at him, her expression, for once, serious. Her eyes almost... weepy. "Your father would have been so proud."

The restless, antsy feeling returned, and the sincerity in her tone only made him feel more on edge. Of course his father would have been proud. *Blake* was proud. But the real question was…why wasn't he happy?

He could touch Jax whenever he wanted. He'd engaged in a hard-fought, satisfying battle in court and won. And he'd just achieved his goal of a promotion. The first step on a path that could take him all the way to the head of the department. He *should* feel happy. But all he felt was this lingering ambivalence.

What the hell was wrong with him?

His mother interrupted his thoughts. "In celebration of your courtroom victory, I made a delicious batch of chocolate scones," his mother said, and Blake's heart groaned even as he bit back the grin, taking in the now forced smiles on Jax's and Nikki's faces.

"Nikki, come to the kitchen and help me with the plates," his mom said.

Blake's smile grew harder to restrain as he watched his mother lead Nikki away, champagne glass in hand again as she shared the supersecret ingredient that would ensure that *this* batch of scones would be better than the flop she'd served them last.

When the two were gone, Jax turned to Blake. "You're on fire, Suit," she said sincerely. "Congratulations."

"Thanks," he said, sorry the celebratory moment didn't quite reach his heart. He took a sip of his bubbly champagne. "Actually, I have more good news."

Jax lifted a brow. "Better than a guilty verdict, a promotion and the promise of your mother's scones?"

Blake's brow bunched in humor at her teasing tone. "This weekend my mother is taking Nikki away for an overnight trip to a spa in West Palm Beach. She told Nikki it's their first annual mother-daughter retreat." He sent Jax a small grin. "She told *me* she's getting Nikki out of the house so we can be alone."

The thought of spending two whole days with Jax without

worrying about the prying eyes of the world was thrilling. The thought of his *future* weighed heavily on his heart. For some reason he couldn't explain, after years of working and planning and sacrificing for this very moment, he didn't want to think about the promotion. Which made no sense, but he pushed the restless feelings aside. Right now he just wanted to enjoy today's hard-earned verdict and the presence of the beautiful, amazing woman by his side.

Now was a time for celebration, and he wasn't going to miss this opportunity with Jax.

"But, as this is my mother, her help comes with a cost, of course," Blake continued. "We have to attend her friend's fundraiser next week. A silent art auction."

"Sounds simple enough."

"Yeah," he said skeptically. "That's what has me worried. But I've decided not to look the gift horse in the mouth."

"Good plan," she said with a smile. "So what did you have in mind for this weekend?"

"A boat trip to the Keys," he said. "There's a beautiful little barrier island where I used to dive for lobster," he said. "Very private. Gorgeous little bay. You game?"

The sound of Abigail's voice from down the hall filled the air, and Jax sent him a small grin. "Will there be baked goods?"

The laugh that escaped Blake's mouth was loud. "No baked goods."

Her grin grew bigger. "Then count me in."

Sprawled on her stomach next to Blake, Jax rested her cheek on her hands, the heat from the sun drying the salt water clinging to her body as she stared out at where aquamarine waters met cornflower-blue sky. The trampoline making up the rear of the catamaran doubled as a comfortable place to rest, the soothing sound of lapping waves lulling her into an almost blissful state of complacency. But despite their idyllic setting, which included a view of the white sandy beach of the tiny barrier island, Blake's eyes and that beautifully sensual mouth showed signs of underlying strain.

Jax worried her lower lip, lost in thought.

In some ways, Blake was the most relaxed she'd ever seen him. Not a suit in sight, just bathing trunks or a breathtaking nakedness as he'd made love to her. And with his recent run of good news, not to mention all of the great sex, why was he looking so pensive?

Was he wondering how he'd wound up in a sexual relationship with a woman who didn't fit his requirements? She'd never be considered sensible or practical. As a matter of fact, Jack had callously called her unstable. And she'd coerced Blake into defending her in court, so law-abiding was a bit of stretch, as well.

Jax let out a quiet sigh, hating the self-doubt. With each passing day, she knew she was at risk of falling too hard for him, the thought more than a little disconcerting. Perhaps now was the time for a little sleuthing.

She pushed aside the beach bag between them and scooted closer to Blake, propping her elbow on the trampoline, head on her hand. "What are you thinking about?"

Lying on his back, he looked up at her, and, after a brief moment, he reached out to brush back a wet strand of hair that clung to her cheek. A lazy grin spread across his lips, doing wonderful things to his handsome face.

But she could tell the smile didn't quite reach his eyes....

"I'm wondering how long I have to wait before I get you naked again," he said, eyeing the cleavage of her one-piece suit.

Predictably, heat flushed through her body in an oh-yes response, but she ignored it. "Nice try, Bathing Suit," she said drolly. "I'm talking about the thoughts that are creating the tension around that skillful mouth of yours."

"Maybe it's just fatigue from making love to you."

Her lips quirked, but she pushed harder. "Liar," she said, because stamina wasn't his problem. Something else was. And she needed to know that it wasn't about her. "Try again."

She met his cool gray gaze with a determined one of her own.

As if sensing there was no escape, he heaved out a small breath and turned his head to stare up at the sky. "I'm thinking about the promotion."

Surprise shot her brow higher, and Jax studied his profile and the sexy stubble on his chin, the moment filled with warm sunshine, the smell of coconut sunscreen and the sight of Blake's lean, muscular torso drying in the sun. Salt water beaded on his chest and stomach, clinging adoringly to the hard abs. Heart tripping faster, she pushed the distracting thoughts aside, because right now she needed to focus on what was causing the worry lines around Blake's eyes.

Something told her they were about more than just a job.

"Did you accept the position?" she said.

His voice was matter-of-fact, logic and reason radiating from his face. "I told them I'd have to think about the offer."

Despite her uneasiness, a teasing smile crept up her mouth. "Of course you did," she said, looking down at him. "Because you always stop to consider your next move from every angle."

And he did, too. Even going so far as to proclaim the first time he'd slept with her as an exception to his rules. He hadn't said anything more on the subject since. Had he simply extended the offer to include more time?

And suddenly, she needed to know if he were capable of letting go of the rules. Would he always be a by-the-book kind of guy? Was she destined to be an exception until he'd gotten his fill of her crazy ways?

She tipped her head. "Do you ever do anything for fun, just because you want to?"

"I used to be famous for it."

She let out a disbelieving laugh. "Back when you were three years old?"

"Up until I turned twenty, I was worse than Nikki," he said, looking up at her again.

Shock drove her eyelids wide. "I don't believe it."

"It's true," he said easily. "Whatever Nikki has done to drive me crazy, I did ten times worse to my father. High school was one trip to the principal's office after another."

Her disbelief must have been obvious, because he shifted to face her, his head propped on his hand. But a part of her was afraid to believe there might be hope for the man.

She narrowed her eyes at him. "I want an example."

"Okay," he said. His eyes crinkled in humor. "My sophomore year in high school, I put a gator in the pool at school."

She sat up, shock dropping her mouth open.

"The alligator was only three feet long," he went on, ignoring her stunned look. "But the coach ignored my hastily scribbled Do Not Feed the Gator sign and didn't see him until he was halfway into the water. And just for the record," he went on drily, "it's impossible to back up from a swan dive."

The image made her laugh. "And then what happened?"

"Swim practice was canceled, just as I'd hoped. At least until Fish and Wildlife fished the gator out and released him back into the wild."

"No," she said with an amused shake of her head. "What happened to *you*?"

"My dad spoke with the principal and got my suspension cut from ten days to three. He constantly had to use his negotiating skills to bail me out of trouble." A glimmer of a nostalgic smile lifted his lips. "By my senior year, the pranks got a little of hand."

She stared at him, trying to take it all in. The image didn't gel with the Blake she knew. She'd always assumed Nikki was like her mother, while Blake had the steadfast genes of his father. But perhaps there was more of Abigail Bennington in him than she'd originally thought.

And the possibility brought a surge of hope so strong it scared her.

"So what happened to ruin you?" she said.

"Most people would say I grew up." His eyes crinkled in genuine amusement. "Leave it to Jacqueline Lee to say I've been ruined."

She fought the need to let the conversation continue at a lighter level. To keep the tone easy and fun. But as she stared across at him, she felt an intense need to be honest. If Blake Bennington couldn't learn to loosen up a bit, if he couldn't relax those so-called compatibility rules—because no one would *ever* consider Jax sensible—then their relationship was just a succession of one-night-stand aberrations.

With no chance for more.

Her sincerity was reflected in her tone. "I think you take caution to unhealthy levels."

His eyes flickered with an unidentifiable emotion. "A certain amount is necessary."

"Too much is stifling."

"Not enough and you pay a heavy price," he said.

Gazes locked, several seconds passed by, until Blake broke the silence. "Case in point, one night I was out with two of my college buddies when we got picked up by the police. We'd handcuffed three guys from a rival fraternity to a statue down at South Point Park."

"You're kidding me." She blinked back her concerns, loving the snapshots of the hell-raiser Blake from his youth. Encouraged by his stories, the tension easing a bit, she stretched out beside him again. "Why did you do that?"

"Retribution." He sent her a rueful smile. "They'd loosened the bolts on our derby car earlier that day, and it fell apart during our annual fundraiser race. The wreck was pretty spectacular," he said with an amused grimace. "They were drinking heavily in celebration of their victory, which was why it was so easy to handcuff them to that statue." He let out a soft grunt. "We weren't completely sober ourselves."

"I can't picture you in police custody."

"Dad came down, smoothed everything out and got them to drop the charges." His mouth tipped up on one side. "It was handy having a powerful and influential father."

"Did the incident make him angry?"

The pause was short. "It made him dead."

The words barreled into her with enormous force, and she sucked in a breath, her chest hurting. Her heart pounding. She'd thought the price he'd paid had been his run-in with the police. His almost arrest. But she'd been wrong.

Terribly, terribly wrong.

With tremendous effort, she swallowed back the horror-stricken look.

When Blake went on, his voice was low. "If he hadn't had to come pick me up, we wouldn't have been out on the road at two in the morning when that car crossed the median."

Pain cinched harder around her chest, and Jax bit back the need to touch him, to comfort him. During their previous discussion of his father's wreck, not once had he mentioned he'd been in the car. Or that he'd been present when his father had died. She'd experienced a lot of painful losses in her life, but had never had to witness the death of a loved one.

"All I got was a cut from flying glass," he said, his expression almost blank as he leaned back and touched the scar on his eyebrow, and the ache in her chest grew tighter. "My dad didn't look or act too injured, either, but I learned later he was bleeding into his brain."

Jax blinked back the sting in her eyes, her heart bleeding for *him*.

Blake cleared his throat, staring up at the sky, his face impassive. "He must have known something was wrong, though. He kept telling me I had to start taking my future seriously.

That I had to take care of Nikki and my mother." He let out a self-accusatory huff. "So I promised I would, but I kept telling him to quit being a worrier, to lighten up because he was going to be fine." After another pause, he rolled his head and looked at her. "But he died. And my family lost a great husband and father," he said. "And Florida lost one of the best United States attorneys this state has ever seen."

Given the tragedy, his gaze was remarkably steady on hers, but the deep sadness and regret in his tone was heartbreaking. So much more than just her future with Blake was at stake. His happiness appeared to be at risk, as well.

She blinked back the tears that threatened on his behalf. "Are you trying to take his place?"

He shot her a skeptical look. "I couldn't even if I wanted to," he said. "But working my way up the system has been my goal since I first joined the Department of Justice."

If so, why wasn't he more excited about the promotion? She'd sensed his inner turmoil since their boat trip began, and now she knew it was in response to the job offer. Which should have made her feel better, but now she felt worse. Because after hearing how his dad had died, it was obvious he was still trying to live up to the promise he'd made to his father.

But no good could come from living your life trying to fill a dead man's shoes.

"I'd be a fool not to accept the new position," he said.

"Forget what other people think." She longed to get him to see reason. The kind of reason that involved the heart, not just the head. "What do *you* want?"

The pause that followed felt as though it lasted forever, and she could see the doubt etched on his face.

"I like the excitement of the chase of the investigation," he said slowly. "I enjoy the challenge of the trials. But the higher up the chain I go, the less hands-on the position will become." His eyes honest, he gave a small shrug. "I'm happy where I am."

"Then turn the offer down."

He pressed his lips together. "It's a big opportunity," he said, his tone pure logic. "I'd be a fool to pass it up."

Looking down at him, Jax sent him a pointed lift of a brow. "Is that you talking?" she said. His expression was more conflicted than she'd ever seen, and her voice dropped an octave, desperate to get through to Blake. "Or your father?"

The flicker in his eyes reflected the truth in her words.

Blake rolled his head to stare up at the sky again, his voice distant. "It's hard to tell the difference anymore."

Jax studied his profile, struggling for the words that would convince him to let the heavy weight of responsibility go. But she was experienced enough to know that those words might not exist, because although the car accident hadn't left Blake with massive scars on the outside, he carried them heavily on the inside.

And as Jax had learned long ago, those were the hardest to heal.

A look she couldn't interpret flashed through his eyes, and his breath came out in a frustrated whoosh. "And here I am, whining about my past, when you—"

Jax covered his mouth with her hand. She knew what he'd been about to say.

"This isn't a competition," she said, sending him a softly chastising look.

No way was she going to let him belittle his past by mentioning hers, as if his suffering had somehow been less significant in comparison. Pain was pain, no matter how it was served. And his certainly affected his choices for the future.

The sensual lips beneath her fingers sent a skitter of desire down her limbs. She had no idea how long her time with him would last. And she was hit with an overwhelming need to bury her worries about where he was headed, where *they* were headed, and simply make love to him again—both the former hell-raiser and the current rule-follower.

Her lips quirked into a gently teasing smile. "But if we're comparing our physical scars..." Jax sat up and slid the straps of her one-piece down to her hips, exposing her skin and the numerous marks on her belly. She sent him her best sultry look, knowing he'd get distracted by her bared breasts. He *always* got distracted by her bared breasts. "My scars are definitely more impressive than yours."

As predicted, heat flared in his eyes as they traveled down her curves.

His voice husky, he said, "Is *this* a competition?"

"If it was, you'd lose."

She sent him her best seductive smile, and his sexy gaze lit a fire low in her belly, only to be tinctured by the burn of something else when his gaze landed on her abdomen.

Her breathing grew shallow, quick, as she willed herself not to move. They'd made love multiple times since that day she'd revealed her scars to him, but anytime he'd tried to touch one, she'd moved his hand to more important, more needy areas. Hoping to sidetrack his efforts.

But he'd talked so frankly about his own wounds, the least she could do was let him *look* at hers. And the moment was going well, until he reached out to touch one, and her heart dropped to her toes....

CHAPTER TEN

DESPITE THE HESITATION on her face, Blake didn't budge as he looked up at Jax, his finger resting on her largest scar.

When she'd pulled her suit down to her waist, he was positive she hadn't been thinking about having another serious conversation, much less one about *her* past. He forced his gaze to remain on her hazel eyes, though he longed to linger on her bared chest. If he'd been a weaker man, her distraction would have worked.

He swallowed hard, hoping he wasn't a weaker man.

With effort, Blake dropped his gaze past the lovely, enticing curves of her breasts to the permanent marks covering her belly, rubbing the ridge of flesh beneath his finger. The moment stretched, a seagull calling overhead, and Jax shifted, as if growing uncomfortable.

She nodded at the scar he traced, the shape resembling the number sign on a computer keyboard. "You can play tic-tac-toe on that one," she said casually, as if to lighten the moment.

"When did you make it?"

"On my fourteenth birthday," she said, and his heart contracted so hard it physically hurt.

So young.

And it didn't take much to realize how lonely that birthday must have been for her.

He reached out to grip her hip. "Jesus, Jax—"

"It's okay," she said, covering his hand with hers as if he were the one that needed comforting.

Five seconds passed as she returned his gaze, her eyes remarkably calm.

"The week before was the first time I ever cut myself, and I made the marks on my arm. Which was a huge mistake," she said, as if sensing his need to know more. "The school noticed the wounds and notified my foster parents. And the next thing I knew they were freaking out and wanted me gone." She inhaled slowly, the moment filled with the sound of the sail fluttering in a warm breeze. "I think they were afraid I'd do something really crazy...like hurt one of their kids."

A curse escaped his lips on her behalf, harsher than he'd intended, and a fatalistic smile lifted her lips as she went on.

"Most folks don't understand," she said with a resigned acceptance. "They think you're an attention seeker. Or worse, that you've gone mad." She lifted an eyebrow. "*Unstable* was the expression my boyfriend used when he saw my scars." The cruel word made Blake wince, but Jax gave a tiny lift of her shoulder. "People just react out of fear," she said simply, as if she'd come to grips with the truth long ago.

And he hated that she'd had to learn to tolerate such a grim reality. A boyfriend was bad enough, but family? Family was supposed to protect you, to be on your side no matter what.

They certainly should never turn you away.

The twist on his heart torqued harder, and he sat up, emotion making his voice gruff. "You are the most grounded person I know."

Though he spoke the truth, his words felt so inadequate.

"Thank you," she said softly as she leaned back on her hands, legs extended.

He was pleased she hadn't attempted to cover her scars again. But the frustration, the unfairness of all she'd suffered, burned through him. While he'd been dreaming of peeking down his teacher's blouse and getting into trouble with his friends, she'd been wrestling with a horrendous secret.

"No one should grow up like that," he said.

Jax sent him a small smile, as if trying to ease the reality of her past. "I've come a long way since those days. In high school, I found the teen center, and a music therapist taught me how to play the guitar. I graduated, received counseling in college and landed my dream job." She followed that statement up with another tiny shrug. "Happy ending."

A happy ending…

Palm on her hip, he studiously ignored the soft skin beneath his hand, the desire coursing through his veins. She was an extraordinary woman. Yet despite her indomitable will and her amazing ability to bounce back, there was a lingering sense of disconnect between the self-assured female who was confident of her choices…and the insecurity about her sexuality. He sensed it every time they made love.

And now was the time to change that.

Blake leaned forward and placed his lips on her neck, enjoying the responding catch of her breath and her melting sigh. Her pulse throbbed beneath his mouth. Desire clamping hard in his groin, he closed his eyes against his pounding need in deference to hers, moving his mouth lower to her collarbone.

He skimmed his fingers down to her one-piece, and Jax leaned back and lifted her hips, aiding him in his efforts as he slid the fabric the rest of the way off.

"Good call, Suit," she murmured, as if she were glad he was dropping the subject.

But he wasn't.

Heart pulsing, he tossed the suit aside and stared at Jax. Naked, breathless and clearly anticipating another wild ride, she stared up at him with a heated gaze that definitely tested his status as a weaker man. And then she parted her legs.

For him.

With concerted effort, he subdued the urge to take her. To

stake his claim. Instead, he strove to be the better man. To prove that she was gorgeous, inside *and* out. He traced the largest welt on her abdomen, the one shaped like a tic-tac-toe grid, and she tensed beneath him. Her pulse throbbed even harder in her neck.

Flat on her back, she lifted a brow. "Tic-tac-toe isn't the game I had in mind when you pulled off my suit."

Despite the glimmer of concern in her eyes, she was clearly trying to keep her tone nonchalant. He ignored her attempt to keep it light and shifted down her body, his lips landing on the angrily puckered, permanent welt.

A hiss of frustration—laced with a hint of confusion— whooshed from her lips.

Moving his mouth across her belly, her muscles tense beneath his tongue, he traced the long length of the scar with his lips and placed a hand between her legs. In response, goose bumps peppered her flesh and her body began to relax, the tension easing from her muscles. Encouraged, he began to place imaginary *X*'s with his tongue and *O*'s with open-mouthed kisses, concentrating on the mark she'd carved on her fourteenth birthday.

"Nobody wins at tic-tac-toe," she said, her voice notably breathless.

He looked up at her, noting the flush of desire on her cheeks.

His words came out as a satisfied rumble. "Oh, I'm winning all right."

A sultry smile slipped up her face, and she threaded her fingers through his damp hair as she arched her back again, and need twisted hard inside him. With her hands, she urged his head lower, almost writhing beneath him now.

"Fun and games are over," she said. "It's time to get serious."

"Not yet."

And he'd never been more serious in his life.

He eased his fingers into the silken heat between her legs, and Jax bit her lower lip and groaned.

"Yes," she breathed, almost in relief.

His tongue continued to trace the marks on her belly, blazing a trail as he dedicated himself to tasting every scar on her torso. And when she whispered something to the effect that she'd die if he didn't end her agony soon, his thumb brushed hard across her nub. Jax whimpered.

Sweat broke out at the nape of his neck, but not from the heat of the sun on his back. He knew she wanted him inside her. And his body screamed to give her exactly that. It was what they both wanted. Longed for. *Craved.*

But, damn it, he would be the stronger man. Even if it killed him.

Mouth on her scarred skin, hand between her legs, he drove her higher, enjoying the return of the tension in her abdomen, because this time the strain was due to pleasure. As he brought her closer to the edge, her groans grew louder as she rocked her hips in time with his hand.

Until finally, he firmly flicked his thumb across her nub, and she arched her back, taking the fall.

"Blake," she called, clutching his shoulders as her muscles clenched around him.

While the aftershocks of Jax's orgasm continued, Blake kept one eye on the beautiful sight as he quickly retrieved a condom from the beach bag and shucked his swim trunks, sheathing himself before shifting up her body. Caught up in the overwhelming need to capture a little of her indomitable spirit, to attain a bit of her amazing fortitude for himself, he cupped her face and thrust deep, burying himself in her wet, welcoming warmth.

The morning she received the fabulous news that the rap star Bulldog had decided to sponsor the South Glade Teen

Center music program, Jax threw up for the third time in as many days.

One episode was easy to dismiss as a fluke. With two, she'd prayed hard it was the beginning of a debilitating stomach flu. But three times, without the rest of the symptoms of a virus, could only mean one thing.

Heart pounding, one hand propped against the bathroom wall of the guest cottage, Jax tightened her grip around the phone. A phone still pressed against her chest from her attempt to block the sound of her breakfast making a surprise reappearance. As Jax grappled with the ominous implications, her mind spun. But she was mostly busy struggling to keep her wobbly knees from collapsing. Holding an intelligent conversation with Blake's mother at the same time was really asking too much.

"Jax?" Abigail's muffled voice called out from the phone, "Are you still there? What was that horrible sound?"

Me. Upchucking. Because I think I'm pregnant with your son's baby.

Good God, did the Fates love to stir things up or what? A week ago Blake had kissed her scars, and at first she'd been desperate for him to do something, *anything*, other than lavish attention on the part of her body that, every day, was a reminder of her past. But his mouth had been soothing, reassuring, and his touch between her legs had set her on fire. Burning away the last of her resistance, as if proving she were beautiful, scars and all.

He'd given her a gift. Because now when she looked in the mirror, instead of unhappy memories, she could choose to remember her time with him. Darkness replaced with light. Pain replaced with pleasure.

Who could resist such a fantastic deal?

Even better, since their return from their trip to the Keys last week, Blake had been coming to the guest cottage every night. Life had been the best ever.

Hence the reason, Jax was sure, the Powers that Be had deemed it couldn't last.

Jax lifted the phone back to her ear, remembering Blake's mother was expecting an explanation for the awful sound of her vomiting. "Sorry, Abigail." She pinched the bridge of her nose. "I was straining mightily to move the couch," she said, wincing at the lamest lie ever.

"And what was the splattering noise afterward?"

Jax closed her eyes. "I spilled my cup of tea in the process," she lied again and then cleared her throat, forcing herself to remain coherent despite her panic.

At least for the remainder of the phone call.

Jax scrambled to return to their previous conversation. "How did your friend get Bulldog on board?" Jax asked.

"Franklin sent him the YouTube video of your flash-mob dance," Abigail said, happy to go on with the good news of her musical coup. "He was seriously impressed with your group's talents and the work you do at South Glade. He attended a similar teen club while growing up in Miami." Jax could almost hear the pleased smile in Abigail's voice. "And it didn't hurt that your routine at the courthouse was set to his latest hit."

Though it was heartfelt, Jax's return smile felt weak. "This really is good news, Abigail. I couldn't have raised the funding without you." Her heart softened and her lids stung with emotion. "You're the best."

"Don't worry, Jax. You can return the favor sometime," Abigail said, and Jax's stomach rebelled at the thought of trying Abigail's peppermint scones. "And speaking of favors," Blake's mother continued, "don't forget my friend's breast-cancer benefit starts tonight at eight. I'll have her leave yours and Blake's tickets at the door."

At the reminder of the event they'd promised to attend in exchange for a weekend alone, Jax smothered her groan. How would she manage an evening in a floor-length gown while suppressing the urge to toss her cookies? All the while accompanied by the father of the baby, the man who had no idea he was a father. And would Blake prefer that the mother of his kids be litigator Sara? The lady who was reasonable and practical and sane? The one who could pull off fractional children with perfection?

Jax's stomach roiled again, and she pressed her lips together, wondering if she would last through the incubation of a whole one.

A baby.

Heart rate escalating, she forced herself to focus on the rest of the conversation with Abigail. After a little more talk about the benefit, the dress Jax had bought to wear and how to move forward with Bulldog's offer—none of which penetrated her preoccupied thoughts—Jax signed off. She blew out a breath, relieved she'd survived the call, and tossed the phone onto the couch. Desperate for a retreat, she padded barefoot down the hall and into her bedroom, flopping onto her bed. The covers were still rumpled from last night's activities with Blake as she stared up at the ceiling, a single word echoing in her thoughts.

Pregnant.

She blinked and fought to control her heart rate, struggling to sort out her jumbled emotions. Fear. Apprehension. Confusion. There was plenty to go around. And the feeling of inadequacy clamped hard around her throat. But mixed in with all of the racing thoughts was a tiny bud of intense hope. Of happiness.

Joy.

Jax pressed her lids closed, fighting the urge to contain the emotion. In an attempt to self-soothe, she placed a hand on her belly, absently rubbing the scars that Blake had traced while making love to her. Somewhere beneath her marked-up skin was her son or daughter. A little imp already bound and determined to make its presence known. Her lips quirked, and Jax could no longer fight the feeling of elation.

Because her only living relative had died the day death had claimed her grandmother. For the first time in what felt like forever, there was someone on this planet who was connected to her, always—in a genetic bond that was unbreakable. She gave a watery sniff, her hand stroking her belly.

Just remember that when you hit those hellacious adolescent years, kid.

She inhaled a breath, her smile winning out over the emotional, overly hormonal state that had her teetering on the edge of tears. She had been petrified of feeling at home with Blake's family, carefully pushing aside the growing sense of belonging for fear the beautifully realized dream—the one she'd given up on long ago—would be taken away, leaving her to deal with another crippling loss. And now, if nothing else, Nikki and Abigail would be a permanent part of Jax's life, the baby sealing them as a forever family.

Jax dragged a less-than-steady hand through her hair, drawing strength in the knowledge she finally had support, affection, love...

But what about Blake?

Her heart flip-flopped in her chest. Up until now, she'd been afraid to think beyond next week, because their rocky start and his list of dating requirements had made a permanent relationship unlikely. Concentrating on the present and burying thoughts of a future had been the safest route to take.

But time, and now a baby, had made that impossible. Blake would never walk away from his responsibilities. But could he learn to love her?

Don't you dare expect too much, Jax.

The surge of apprehension was strong. The clear plastic covering that coated her heart, several layers thick after her years in foster care and Jack's desertion, was growing weaker by the minute.

When another sting of tears returned, she pushed them aside.

No blubbering like a baby, Jax. It's warrior time. The little imp needs you to be strong.

Scrubbing her hand across her eyes, impatient with the weepy feelings, she made her plans. First, she'd confirm her condition. No sense in bothering with an over-the-counter test. If it was positive—and she knew in her heart, her gut and every other anatomical part that she was pregnant—then she wanted to see her family-practice doctor ASAP. If the test was negative, then she wanted to get to the bottom of the annoying vomiting anyway.

Either way, the day started with a call to her doctor.

And since she had no intention of spending the evening at some benefit wondering when and how she was going to share the news with her baby's father, that meant the second call she had to make was to Blake.

Anxiety rolled through her and she held her stomach again, willing the little imp to behave…at least until she'd called its father.

CHAPTER ELEVEN

"I DON'T UNDERSTAND how this could have happened." Looking stunned, Blake paced Dr. Murphy's small office. A last-minute cancellation had left Jax scrambling to make it to the appointment in time, and Blake had insisted on meeting her here. "We always used a condom," he said.

Jax hadn't seen this kind of pacing since Blake had discovered the truth about her virginity, disturbed he'd hurt her in the process of making that particular condition a thing of the past. And, by the expression on Dr. Murphy's face as she sat on the other side of her walnut desk, the middle-aged redhead looked as if she'd battened down the hatches for a tumultuous encounter.

But his back-and-forth motion was making Jax dizzy. "Would you please just relax and sit down?" Jax said, patting the empty chair beside her.

"But I don't understand how," Blake repeated, clearly not referring to the process of sitting.

Instead of answering right away, Dr. Murphy again watched Blake cross her small office—a room that was insufficient for his long legs and the to-and-fro motion. The physician looked prepared to wait for him to work off a little frenetic energy before trying to get him to listen to reason.

He didn't look angry.

He didn't look trapped.

He looked like a man who'd been thrown a huge curveball he had no idea how to catch.

And Jax realized it was the second time in their relationship where it was up to her to be the one to remain calm and not fall apart. Her heart squeezed in her chest, softening at the adorable sight of a flustered Blake, the vulnerable look on his face endearing. Jax was thrilled with the out-of-control demeanor from the man who had an irritating tendency to be rational every moment of the day.

And his description of their activities wasn't entirely accurate, so Jax said, "Well, we didn't use a condom *every* time."

"Yes, we did." Blake stared at Jax as he passed by. "I was there, remember?"

She squelched the urge to roll her eyes. "Of course I do."

Jax opened her mouth to go on, but Dr. Murphy chose that moment to join the discussion. "Then the pregnancy is most likely due to a condom failure," the doctor said.

"Condom failure?" Blake almost looked offended. "I didn't skimp. I chose a quality product."

Jax was amazed Dr. Murphy managed to maintain a straight face. "I'm sure your condoms were of the finest quality," the doctor said soothingly, and Jax pressed her lips together to subdue a smile.

Blake finally stopped pacing and turned to look at the physician, who wore a forbearing expression that screamed, "Lord, save me from the clueless male."

Jax cleared her throat, determined to finish her previous statement. "But as I'm sure you remember," she said drily, looking at Blake, "the first time we…" Jax shifted her gaze to Dr. Murphy, who was eyeing her patiently, and searched for a delicate way to phrase the particulars of the story. "The first time, we got caught up in the moment," she finished with a defeated shrug.

For a brief second, the reasonable, rational lawyer returned, and Blake didn't flinch at the overshare. "But I didn't finish until the condom was in place."

"But if there was unprotected entry during the excitement phase," Dr. Murphy went on matter-of-factly, and Jax fought the urge to cringe at the clinical description, "it's possible this could be the result of pre-ejaculate."

Blake's expression was that of a man who was used to being in control…but was now in way over his head. Drowning, in fact.

Jax's heart twisted a little harder. He really was adorable when he was suffering and under the gun.

"In the literature, there is some debate as to whether or not the fluid in pre-ejaculate contains sperm," Dr. Murphy continued, and Blake looked as if he'd just been scooped up and plopped down into the nether regions of hell, but the good doctor went on calmly. "Some studies failed to find any, yet others confirm their presence. In a limited quantity, of course."

Jax cleared her throat and finally found her voice. "Of course," she said. "Interesting information. Makes you wonder what other kinds of studies are going on."

Apparently Blake wasn't appreciating the amusement in the moment.

Obviously unperturbed, Dr. Murphy continued with her no-nonsense tone of voice. "But it is entirely feasible that, if an orgasm occurred prior to entry, there would be viable sperm left in the urethra to be released with the pre-ejaculate."

Jax sat up straight, the news surprising. She knew without a doubt that Blake had not been fooling around with another woman before he'd come to her, so to speak.

She sent Blake a wide-eyed look. "Okay, but if he had an orgasm before our first time together, then he did it without me," Jax said.

The impassive look on Blake's face was impressive. "My

last relationship ended well over six months ago," Blake said firmly. "Jax is the only woman I've had sex with since."

Dr. Murphy's cool demeanor didn't change. "But that doesn't discount the possibility of masturbation," she said, and Jax coughed, choking back a shocked gasp.

Jeez, Dr. Murphy isn't pulling her punches anymore.

Jax forced the smile from her mouth, expecting an instant denial from Blake. Instead, the tint of color in Blake's cheeks was obvious, and realization slowly dawned.

Dr. Murphy had just nailed the pre-ejaculate-sperm conundrum.

And Blake's discomfort, his endearing blush and his abject helplessness broke the rest of the clear coating covering Jax's heart. There was no denying the truth anymore.

She was head over cowboy heels in love with Blake Bennington.

Her heart rate escalated and her breathing became erratic, her stomach churning. The fear she'd felt when she'd first worried about Blake's reaction now gave way to sheer, absolute terror. Bile rose in the back of her throat, putting her previous bouts of morning sickness to shame.

Love.

She was *in love* with Blake.

Jax splayed her hand across her abdomen, heart thumping in her ears, willing herself to remain calm. At least until she was alone and could come unglued properly.

Dr. Murphy typed something into her laptop. "Jax, I don't need to see you back for another month. And your prescription for prenatal vitamins will be available at the pharmacy by the end of the day." She gave Jax a reassuring smile, but Jax's answering smile felt weak. Dr. Murphy turned to Blake and eyed him warily. "Do you have any more questions, Mr. Bennington?"

Jax was impressed with the woman's how-far-are-you-willing-to-take-this-conversation? tone in her voice. Apparently Blake had decided to quit while he was lagging so far behind.

Blake took her elbow and escorted her out the door and down the hall, past a wall with pictures of ovaries and wombs and babies lining the wall. He carefully kept his eyes in front, as if afraid to take in the decor, and, despite the terror still swelling inside, her heart grew softer still.

She really shouldn't be so charmed by Blake's display of vulnerability. Or so enchanted by the chink in his rational armor. And she certainly shouldn't be entertained by the sight of the man so clearly out of his element. But it was strangely soothing to see him so disconcerted, because it would wreak havoc on her nerves to be the only one falling apart. In her current state of panic, of being in *love*, she couldn't handle the logical Blake.

So it was best to keep him as off-kilter as she felt.

"Is it true?" she asked, her wide-eyed innocent look masking the chaos inside.

He kept his eyes ahead. "Is what true?" he said, his tone even.

But it was the slight tightening of his fingers on her elbow that gave him away. He knew well and good the question she was about to ask.

"Before coming to see me that first night," she said. "You arrived home from a hard day's work and decided to relax with a beer and a little self-indulgent...touching?"

The grim set to his jaw and the return of a hint of color to his cheeks were all the answer she needed, and Jax was amazed she managed to restrain the very immature laugh that threatened to bubble from her mouth.

Or maybe fear was responsible for her teetering on the edge of hysterics.

Without a word, Blake led her past the receptionist's desk and into the waiting room that contained two kids with their mother and several women with varying stages of baby bumps. They passed one with a belly the size of the Grand Canyon, and Jax thought Blake was going to have a nervous breakdown right then and there.

Jax understood the feeling well. She was in love with a man whose top three dating requirements precluded her as a girlfriend. So how the heck did he feel about her as the mother of his *baby*?

It became apparent Blake had no intention of responding to her inquiry regarding his secret jerking off. "How's your vision?" she said as innocently as she could, feeling particularly evil. "Have you gone blind yet?"

His only answer was a give-me-a-break tightening of his lips.

She didn't bother keeping her voice down as she continued to harass the man. "Was it as good for you as it was for yourself?"

The look he shot her was harsh, but he remained mute.

And since Blake refused to answer her admittedly ridiculous questions, Jax went on, keeping her voice just low enough to be considered a whisper. "Were you thinking of me when you were having sex with yourself?"

He held the front door open for her, and she skimmed past him, brushing close. This time the look he sent her was filled with heat, and not the angry kind. Need uncoiled inside her, the sensual sensation overpowering now that she'd admitted to herself that she was in love. Jax's heart thumped with lust and love and *fear* as he finally answered one of her questions.

His eyes dark, he raked a carnal look down her body, setting her on fire. "I damn sure wasn't thinking of Mother England."

In the back of the limo, Jax leaned close to redo the tie of Blake's tux. He dreaded the benefit auction tonight, because his mind hadn't stopped spinning since she'd called him this morning with the life-altering news. Breathing was difficult.

Completing the complicated task of securing a bow knot had been impossible.

Because, to hell with going blind, who would have guessed that masturbation could lead to fatherhood?

He still couldn't wrap his brain around the turn of events, especially given how Jax looked. Adorned in a red, floor-length spaghetti-strap dress that emphasized her cleavage, she wasn't exactly emitting a motherly vibe. And Blake wondered if his inner turmoil was visible on his face.

He was going to be a father....

Blake's stomach lurched.

As she fixed the tie around his neck, Jax said, "You were a little crooked, Suit."

Crooked? He'd been turned completely inside out.

He inhaled the smell of spiced apricots, every one of his senses feeling heightened. Most likely because of the pure, pumping rush of shocked adrenaline that continued to surge through his veins.

He was going to be a *father.*

The weight of responsibility consumed him, leaving room for little else. Not that he hadn't planned on one day getting married. Perhaps even having a few kids. But that had been far into the future, not an immediate possibility.

"Are you done freaking out?" she said.

Hardly. He was just getting started.

Instead, he said, "I did not freak out."

"Yes, you did," she said with a small laugh. "Admit it. You had a complete and total meltdown." The glimmer in her eyes was lighthearted, but beneath he detected a note of concern. Probably because she figured his meltdown was ongoing. "In your own adorable way, of course," she said.

He studied her for a moment before responding, his voice honest. "This wasn't how I pictured starting a family."

Her fingers stilled at his neck, and then she dropped her

hands to her lap. "The best things in life are rarely planned," she said lightly, her expression wary.

But, planned or not, the baby was his. The *responsibility* was his. And he kept hearing his father's voice in his head, telling Blake he had to step up and be accountable for his actions.

You have to start taking your future seriously, Blake.

You have to stop thinking only of yourself and start thinking about your family.

Heart buckling at the memory, he let the words slip. "We need to plan the wedding."

Jax's hand paused in the midst of brushing a strand of wild, tawny hair from her cheek, and she met his gaze head-on. "There'll be plenty of time for that later," she said simply.

Blake refused to frown at her hesitation. "I suspect the next eight months are going to fly by."

She finally tucked the lock behind her ear and smoothed her hand down her dress. "We can get married after the baby is born."

He sensed the words for what they were: a delaying tactic. The idea of waiting cut against the grain, and Blake twisted in his seat, studying Jax carefully as the sense of dissatisfaction settled deep.

"We have to get married before," he said.

The look on Jax's face was hardly encouraging. "Says who?"

Blake opened his mouth, but no words came out, his mind scrambling for an answer that didn't sound antiquated and dated. Society? Their family?

Convention?

The thought in regard to Jax was laughable, so he gave up and frowned. "I said."

Jax lifted her eyebrows, an almost eye-roll that clearly communicated she thought his excuse was lame. "I refuse to give my wedding a shotgun theme."

Unhappy with the turn of events, he pressed his lips together as the limo pulled up to the curb in a trendy section of town.

"No one is using any weapons here," Blake said, struggling to keep the frustrated tone from his voice.

The driver opened the door, cutting off further conversation, and Jax stepped out. Blake fought to control the profound sense of unease and followed her onto the sidewalk. He took her arm and led her up the steps to the beautiful modern building hosting the benefit, surprised by the sign out front. He supposed reconstructive surgery was the connection, but a plastic surgeon's office hardly seemed the usual location to hold a fundraiser, even for breast cancer.

Nothing about this evening was going as expected.

Blake ushered her through the glass doors, and, as they passed into the posh lobby full of guests and paintings on display for the silent auction, he tried again. "It's clearly in the best interest of the baby if we—"

She turned and laid a hand on his chest, gazing up at him with steady hazel eyes. "Look around you," Jax said in a reasonable tone as she gestured at the luxurious surroundings, the hardwood floors and stainless-steel accents, giving it more of a luxurious-spa feel than one of a man who made women's breasts bigger for a living. "Tonight we are going to have a nice time," she said. "We can talk about this later."

But for the next hour and forty-five minutes, the worries settled deeper, embedding their way into his every thought. Jax looked beautiful in her gown, wild hair tumbling down her back, but as she chatted easily with the guests, his disturbing feelings grew to monumental proportions. The silent auction of a renowned artist's work on women's health issues went on around him, but he felt detached. Distanced. He shot a glance at an oil painting of a woman getting a mammogram—and who would pose for such a thing?—and he wondered if the only way the artist could sell the portrait was to benefit a charity.

"I like this one," Jax said, studying the oil of women in various stages of pregnancy. She sent him a teasing, tentative grin. "All that's missing are a few pacing males."

Blake shot her a wry look and was just about to lay out his argument in favor of marrying sooner rather than later when he was interrupted by a woman's voice.

"Blake!"

He turned and watched his mother's friend approach. Gail Taylor was a too-slim blond, fiftysomething social-ite who looked as if she'd indulged in the facility's breast-augmentation offerings. She greeted Blake with a smile, and he introduced her to Jax.

"Oh, yes," Gail said to Jax, her genuine smile growing big-ger. "I saw the news clip with that rap star. The one starting a fund to continue the music program at the club for teens. Congratulations."

Jax's face grew more radiant. "Thank you," she said. "I'm really looking forward to getting back to work."

She ignored, of course, that he had to get the charges against her dropped before she could return. But as usual, Jax didn't seem concerned with the details.

The blonde woman leaned in conspiratorially, her voice an octave lower. "I heard a volunteer at the club got mugged on her way back to her car recently," Gail said. Blake's heart thumped harder at the disturbing piece of news, and the woman went on. "It's hardly the safest of neighborhoods." Her eyebrows lowered in concern. "You should be careful, Jax."

"I've been working there since I finished college. And I was a volunteer for the three years before that." Jax sent her a reassuring smile. "I've never had any trouble."

Jax's expression and the tone in her voice made it clear she was unconcerned. But this was nothing knew, because she rarely concerned herself about anything, even the really important matters. Like pregnancy and marriage.

And ensuring the stability of their baby's future.

He was careful to keep his tone even, but it was a struggle. "One of the volunteers got mugged?"

"Just this week," Gail said. "But she's fine now."

He turned to Jax and lifted a meaningful brow. "Did you know?"

"No," she said, her smile a little tight. "But I'm sure it was no big deal."

"Are you kidding me?" Gail Taylor said, disagreement written all over her face. "She got knocked unconscious. A coworker found her lying on the ground in the parking lot, bleeding from a nasty wound on her head."

The words rose sharply, creating a vivid image that slammed into Blake's gut with the power of a sledgehammer.

An image of his father in the wrecked car.

An image of Jax's pregnant body…sprawled on a parking lot.

Blake's palms grew damp and his vision narrowed, until all he could see was Jax's pink lips moving, changing the topic of conversation with Gail back to Jax's work with the teens. But her face slipped in and out of focus, overlaid by his father's. Gray. Slack.

Lifeless.

His heart thundered in his chest, and sweat broke out on his brow. Nausea bulged, the acid burning his throat as the contents in his stomach threatened to rebel. Knowing he needed time to regain his composure, he muttered an excuse and pivoted on his heel, weaving around people and a portrait of a woman in a paper medical gown as he headed for the men's room.

When he pushed open the door, it hit the wall with a resounding thud. Battling the sick feeling, he strode directly to the sink and clutched the basin, the smooth marble cool under his clammy hands. Heat radiated from his body, the effects of the nausea taking hold.

If he'd eaten earlier, he would have vomited.

Willing his body to hold on, he lifted the stopper on the basin and filled the sink, fighting the adrenaline racking his body as he stared into the swirling water. But it was no use. No matter how hard he tried, all he could see was his father's lifeless face...morphing into the familiar features of Jax.

He splashed cold water on his cheeks, the chilling bite just what he needed to regain control. Drying off with one of the towels provided, he inhaled deeply, forcing a return of logic as he prepared to return to the party. Back to Jax.

And a more firmly laid-out plan to get the woman to see reason.

He found her studying a portrait of a woman sitting on an exam table, sheet covering her lap, starring at the stirrups at the end as if she were about to walk the plank.

The frown on her face was thoughtful. "I don't think I'd want this one hanging on my wall," she said easily, oblivious to the turmoil that had wreaked havoc on his system. "But I was hoping you'd bid on the one of the women in the waiting ro—"

"I don't care about the painting, Jax," he said, cutting her off even as he forced himself to remain calm.

Or at least *appear* calm.

Jax stared at him warily. "What is your problem?"

"Right now," he said, his tone forced as he struggled to keep his voice down, "your stubborn insistence on delaying the wedding is my problem. Not to mention the thought of the mother of my baby spending every day in a less-than-safe side of town."

She slowly turned to face him, as if preparing to do battle, and tipped her head in skeptical disbelief. A full five seconds passed before she spoke.

"A list of rules won't save you, Blake. The world is full of danger."

He swallowed back the scoff, despising the platitude. And the most hated platitude of all?

It was an accident, Blake. Your father's death is not your fault.

"Some neighborhoods are worse than others, and you know it," he said. Just another one of those pesky life details that Jax liked to ignore. "We're a family now and we need to make it official."

She inhaled slowly, clearly struggling to maintain her temper. "Our baby has plenty of family. A mother, a father and a lovely grandmother that will make him or her awful birthday cakes. Not to mention the fact that Nikki will make a wonderful aunt," she said firmly, and then she turned on her heel and headed to the next painting.

And suddenly, a horrific possibility occurred to him. She might not say yes. She might not *ever* say yes. He'd be forced to continue watching her from the sidelines. Jax, with her devil-may-care, to-hell-with-the-risks attitude toward life. Engaging in careless actions that not only led to a probationary status at work, an arrest and legal charges to beat, but also had the potential of getting her killed.

But he was doubly screwed, because now her actions wouldn't just affect Jax—they put their baby at risk as well….

Fear drove Blake to follow her with a determined stride. "Jax," he said as he drew closer. "Why do you refuse to make it legal between us?"

"Look, Suit." She pivoted on her heel to face him. "I've always dreamed of having a family," she said, and her admission launched Blake's frustration to unseen levels. "But—"

"So marry me," he implored.

Her eyes flashed, the fire impressive, and she waited a moment before speaking. "As far as I'm concerned," she said, her voice deceptively low, "I already have an official family." She tilted that stubborn chin of hers, and Blake knew trouble wasn't far behind. "I decided long ago that I do *not* need a man to define the entity. Your mother and sister and our baby are all the family I need," she said and then continued on her path to the next painting.

Stunned, he stared at her retreating back, his previous thought echoing in his head.

She'd never say yes.

Several seconds passed before he had the ability to function enough to catch up with her.

His fear had now reached towering proportions, engulfing his ability to fake composure. "Would you stop walking away from me?" he said as he took her arm, bringing her up short. "And why do you always have to be so damn irrational?"

She turned to face him, the color draining from her cheeks, and an ominous sensation settled low in his spine. Because he was sure their discussion was about to take a turn for the worse.

CHAPTER TWELVE

IRRATIONAL.

The word echoed in Jax's head. Irrational. Or, as her last boyfriend had so tactlessly phrased it, *unstable*.

The word slashed deeper with each reverberation in her brain, draining every drop of blood from her face. Leaving her soul bleeding. Instinctively Jax placed a less-than-steady hand on her abdomen, searching for strength from the scars that represented the hard-fought war she'd waged in the past and won.

The horrendous demons she'd faced and *slayed.*

The larger scars were palpable beneath her silk dress, her baby ensconced protectively somewhere beneath.

Warrior, Jax. You are a warrior.

But right now she didn't feel like one. She'd done her best to keep her disappointment with his unromantic proposal from showing. The one that was all about logic and nothing to do with love. She'd been willing to cut him a little slack, given the baby news was so recent and raw. But, unfortunately, his proposal was rapidly approaching more of a dictate.

And now she was beginning to wonder if his behavior had mostly to do with his worries about her history....

Jax sucked in a breath as she fought for control. "You know," she said, struggling to keep the tremor from her voice, "just because we are having a baby together, it doesn't mean we have to get married." Her lips set, she pulled her arm from his grip. "'Cuz God knows we wouldn't want you to be stuck with an irrational wife."

But her attempt at sarcasm fell far short of the mark.

"Jax," he said, the return of his levelheaded look and matter-of-fact tone grating on her sensitive nerves. "You're being unreasonable."

His ability to sound so rational made her want to scream, and it was a struggle to keep her voice low. "I'm being unreasonable?" she said. "*You're* the one who is trying to dictate when I'll get married. Where I'll work."

And she knew what was driving him now.

Fear.

All along she'd thought he'd accepted her past. The history behind her scars. But it simply took a baby to cut through the facade.

With each passing second, her anger at his attitude climbed higher. But the anger warred with the pain for control of her heart. Her dreams of a happy family crumbling again, right before her eyes. Just when she'd thought she'd found a place to belong.

How many times must she be forced to learn the same lesson?

She briefly squeezed her eyes shut before going on. "And you know what?" she said, a tremor in her voice finally slipping through. "In all the times I fantasized about getting married and having a family of my own, I never once hoped it would be with a man who considered me unstable."

Articulating the words out loud hurt, and pain washed through her, clogging her throat.

"I did *not* say you were unstable," he said, a frown replacing the calm demeanor. "You're putting words in my mouth."

Emotion drove her to take a step closer. "Don't lawyer-speak me," she said, her anger kicking up another notch. "You called me irrational." She planted a fist on her hip. "It isn't much of a leap from one to the other."

"What's wrong with wanting to marry the mother of my baby?"

She stared up at Blake, torn between telling him she'd marry him—because the thought of living without him was awful—and telling him no. Because living with a man who doubted her stability would be torture. She'd had those doubts about herself in the past. She couldn't go down that path again.

Especially not while being escorted along by her husband.

Digging her fingernails into her palm, she sucked in a shaky breath. *Marry me, Jax. I love you, Jax.* Were those ideas such a foreign concept?

"Listen, Suit," she said, struggling to keep the fury from her voice, "if you find it difficult dealing with a woman who is so irrational…" She swallowed against the massive lump in her throat, the agony in her chest twisting tighter. "You shouldn't want to marry me."

A scowl overtook his face. "This conversation would be a lot easier if you would stop comparing me to the people from your past," he said. "I am *not* the one who skipped out when I learned the truth about your scars."

"No," she fired back. "You're the man who's claiming I'm being unreasonable because I'm not letting you call the shots. Because I'm not going along with your stupid rational plans."

"Jax," he said, his expression unyielding, "*I'm* the reason my mother lost her husband. *I'm* the reason Nikki lost her father." A muscle in his jaw bunched, and she could tell he was teetering on the edge of losing control. "I screwed up and got my father killed. And I screwed up and got you pregnant."

She was part of his screwup….

The awful moment expanded, filling every available space in her heart, stealing the rest of the blood from her face.

He stepped closer, his expression dark. "And I am not

going to mess things up for my kid," he said. "I have to make this right."

She blinked back the stinging bite of tears. "Nice, Blake," she said, the tone so heavy it was a wonder she managed to form the words. Her heart so low she knew she'd never recover. "What a way to make me feel wanted."

Knowing that a total loss of mental functioning was near, she turned and headed for the front door. And away from Blake.

But he clutched her elbow, as if to escort her, his expression one of pure frustration. "I didn't mean it like that."

"I think you meant every word," she said, her heart thudding hard beneath her ribs.

"So here's a plan for you, Blake," Jax said, pulling her arm from his hand. "You need to deal with your guilt so you can work out your problems with Nikki. Which would include you easing up and letting her make her own mistakes, so she can *quit* feeling the need to push back. And as far as I'm concerned—"

She sucked in a fortifying breath, because the moment of decision was at hand. And she'd never survive living with a man who doubted her judgment.

"I'll be happy to share custody of the baby, of course," she went on, holding her chin high even as her heart was breaking. "But your mom and Nikki and this baby are all the family I need," she said. "I won't marry you."

The last of Blake's patience evaporated, and he shoved a hand through his hair. "Jax, you are pregnant with my—"

"I don't need your approval," she said, jabbing his chest with her finger. "I don't need you to protect me from myself. And I sure as hell don't need a husband who thinks I'm an unstable mistake." She stared up at him, wondering how a broken heart could still function enough to thunder so violently in her chest. "Obviously your list of rules was right."

Her voice cracked, but her words were firm. "I'm the wrong woman for you."

And with that, she turned on her heel and exited the building.

For the second time in as many weeks, Blake found himself in a doctor's office. Nikki was scheduled to have her cast removed, and, fortunately, the orthopedist's office was nothing like Dr. Murphy's. This time the pictures on the wall were of manly muscles and bones and detailed posters of different joints, the artwork consisting of athletes in beautifully photographed positions of execution. All in all, Blake was pleased with the much more male-friendly environment.

Too bad the rest of his life had fallen apart.

He couldn't sleep, and his concentration at work had been shot to hell. For the first time in several years, Blake had taken a week off. Which would have been nice except for the constant agony of missing Jax.

And his worry about her, the baby and their future…

As they waited for the orthopedist to show, Nikki paced the room on her crutches, which had the unfortunate effect of making Blake more uptight than usual. And her topic of conservation was far from soothing, as well.

"I still don't understand why Jax took off so suddenly," Nikki said, and Blake's heart took a hard nosedive toward the floor. Crutches swinging, followed by the forward lurch of her fire-breathing embellished cast, Nikki went on, disappointment clearly etched on her face. "She looked so upset. And I thought everything would be fine after she'd secured the funding for the club."

It would have been, if he hadn't lost his cool trying to get Jax to see reason. Or if she hadn't been so stubborn, insisting on measuring his actions through the distorted lens of her past. A distorted view that had apparently continued.

Because right after the benefit, she'd phoned and left him

a message at his office, informing him that she didn't want him handling her case. Every call he'd placed to her cell in turn had gone unanswered. Until, petrified she'd show up in court and try to represent herself, he'd called Sara and hired her to finish the legal proceedings.

And he hated being kept out of the loop, with no control.

He pushed aside his turbulent feelings and the crushing panic that lingered, choosing to concentrate on Nikki instead.

"Jax didn't leave because of anything you did, Nikki," Blake said.

"I know," she said reasonably, as if there was no doubt in her mind. But his sister's gray eyes were troubled and far too all-seeing for comfort. She came to a stop in front of him and handed him her crutches, as if preparing to sit down. "Y'all had an argument, didn't you?"

Gripping the handles of the crutches, Blake fought to control his pounding heart and keep the concern from his face. The last thing he wanted to do was discuss his problems with his sister, but she was savvy enough to know that Jax's leaving was his fault. And every time she questioned him, putting her off got harder and harder to do. Until now she seemed determined to find out the truth.

"What was the fight about?" she said.

Blake lifted his gaze to his sister and the eyes that were identical to his, and to their father's. Sooner or later he'd have to tell his family anyway.

Waiting wasn't going to make it any easier.

Bracing for Nikki's reaction, he set the crutches aside. "Jax is pregnant with my baby."

Her swift inhalation was sharp, and the delight on her face would have been amusing if Blake hadn't felt so miserable. "You're going to have a kid?" she said.

The uncertainty of his future with Jax, his future with his baby, tightened into a massive ball that sat in his stomach like deadweight, making breathing difficult and losing his break-fast in an undignified way a very real possibility.

The look on his face must have communicated his thoughts.

After several seconds, Nikki's gaze narrowed in suspicion. "What did you do to screw it up, Blake?"

Blake plowed a hand through his hair and let out a weary sigh. "Why does everyone always assume everything is my fault?"

"Because it usually is," she said calmly, as if the matter had already been decided. "Did you ask her to marry you?"

He winced at the memory. "Sort of."

Nikki let out a snort. "You don't 'sort of' ask a woman to marry you. Now, tell me exactly what happened, and maybe I can help you fix this."

"I told her we had to get married."

Nikki's light punch on his arm was almost hard enough to hurt. "You big doofus," she said. "You *told* her?" Her face incredulous, Nikki let out a groan and sank into the seat beside him. "How unromantic can you get?"

He scrunched up his face with regret. "I didn't mean for it to come out that way. But when she said we didn't have to get married, that you and Mom and the baby were all the family she needed, I—" He blew out a breath, trying to finish without making himself look like a jerk. But that didn't seem possible. "I lost my cool."

He used to be the rational guy who never got flustered in court. So where had his usual composure gone? The man who was cool under pressure? But he knew the answer. He'd been blinded by the sheer terror of the vision of her dead, triggered by the memories of his father. Blake let out a self-derogatory grunt.

So who was letting their past control them *now*?

"So what exactly did you say?" Nikki said.

"I told her to start thinking rationally—"

"Holy guacamole, Blake," Nikki squeaked out. "I can't

believe you told a hormonal lady in her first trimester to start thinking rationally. And this isn't the eighteenth century. People don't have to get married just because they're having a baby together. And for heaven's sake, she isn't some witness you can instruct to stick to the facts. She's a woman," Nikki continued, making Blake feel lower than ever before. "A *pregnant* woman—with all the rights to temporary insanity that go along with the condition. Going all authoritative on her was the absolute wrong thing to do." The look of regret on his face must have been profound, because her face grew sympathetic. "Do you love her?"

Love.

Blake closed his eyes. If he hadn't met Jax, he would be with Sara. And if he'd been dating Sara, right now she'd be trying to convince him to take the promotion. She would have methodically laid out her argument, ultimately concluding he'd be a fool to pass on the opportunity. And eventually he would have agreed and accepted the job that took him away from the excitement of the courtroom, continuing on a path that he now realized had been a noose around his neck since he'd started, slowly tightening over time. Choking him. And making him miserable.

But Jax had dared him to follow his heart.

Jax had set him free....

Blake dropped his elbows to his knees and his head into his hands, staring down at the immaculately polished floor. "Yes," he said. "I love her."

The realization had been lingering at the edges of his consciousness for days, taunting him. Admitting the truth out loud only made the misery worse. "And I blew it, big-time."

Nikki's hand on his back was gentle, and she rubbed soothing circles between his shoulder blades. "I'm sure this is fixable," she said with an overly bright tone, as if forcing the optimism. "You were just doing what comes naturally, taking care of the ones you love." The statement eased the tightness in his chest a bit, and he looked at his sister as she went on. "In your own annoyingly overbearing way, of course." She shot him a small smile. "Even the mighty Blake Bennington is allowed to make mistakes."

Mistakes. Like the one he'd made that had cost them their dad's life. The one that had left his sister fatherless at the age of twelve. Guilt compressed his chest with a painful squeeze.

Her voice turned sober and sincere. "Speaking of mistakes," she said, "after my accident, I should have thanked you for coming to get me from the hospital."

He attempted a light tone, but he wasn't convinced he pulled off the nonchalant manner. "It was no big deal."

"That's not true," she said. "It was a very big deal. Even though you drive me crazy, you've always been there for me. And you know how Mom is…." Her voice tailed off.

Blake studied his sister's face, her expression torn. Instead of finishing her sentence, she finished with a small shrug.

"Yeah," he said gruffly. "I know how Mom is."

Abigail Bennington was full of life and totally lovable, but never dependable. And the one thing a child needed was dependability. He'd done his damndest to make sure he'd provided that for Nikki. But it only seemed fair, since he was the reason she was without a father.

His lungs briefly shut down, making breathing impossible. Despite their differences, Jax was right about him needing to be straight with Nikki.

His sister cleared her throat. "Anyway," she went on, patting his back again, "I could always count on you to bail me out."

The guilt dug deeper, until there was no escape. He had to confess the truth that was eating at him, because he didn't deserve her reassuring pat on the back.

"It's my fault that Dad died," he said.

Nikki's hand on his back stalled as she returned his gaze for a moment, and Blake forgot to exhale. If she was angry at him for robbing her of her father at such a young age—and rightly so—would she ever be able to forgive him?

The longest six seconds of his life passed.

Until Nikki finally dropped her hand and said, "I know what happened that night."

"No, you don't," he said, plowing ahead. "I—"

"I heard you and Mom talking years ago," she said calmly, her eyes steady on his. "The college prank. Your drinking." A ghost of a smile crept up her face. "The police threatening an arrest."

She knew. All along, *she knew.*

Nikki paused, and Blake wondered if he'd ever been able to fool this smart young woman poised on the edge of greatness. Apparently not.

"I'm super proud of the brilliant lawyer you've become, Blake," Nikki said softly. And then her face fell a touch, as if not sure how to continue, but she pressed on anyway. "But—"

The pause was long.

"But...?" he said.

"But I remember how it was when Dad was alive. You used to be fun," she said, and his gut twisted at the sadness in her words. "I just sometimes wish it wasn't an either-or, you know?"

She eyed him soberly with a gaze that reminded him more of his father than ever before, a wisdom he'd never really noticed until now. But perhaps that was because he hadn't been looking hard enough.

Blake stared down at the floor as the moment stretched and he contemplated her words: an either-or.

Lust versus reason.

Need versus duty.

Was there really a reason he couldn't have both? Veins burning with an emotion he refused to examine too closely, the possibilities stretched before him. And wasn't that exactly what Jax had been trying to say that day on the boat?

What happened to ruin you?

Decision made, he returned his gaze to Nikki. "I have one more week until Jax's trial goes to court. Will you help me think of a way to win her back?"

"Of course I will," she said. And then she lifted a chastising brow. "But whatever you do, it better be good."

CHAPTER THIRTEEN

Late for your own trial. Way to go, Jax.

Clutching her Ramones tote, Jax hurried up the courthouse steps, muttering curses under her breath. Starting her day upchucking her breakfast had set her behind schedule. And who could have known it would take fifteen minutes to find an empty parking space? The fact that the spot had been the farthest one from the entrance hadn't helped matters, either.

Jax still felt nauseous as she passed through the courthouse doors and made a beeline for the bank of elevators, stabbing the up button in desperation. Heart tripping too fast for comfort, her palms damp, she tapped her foot, willing the elevator to hurry up. As she watched the numbers descend slowly she suppressed the need to scream in frustration. When the light stopped on the floor above, she let out a groan, glancing down at her watch and wincing. She was already ten minutes behind and she still had to get to the fourth floor.

And, as if being late to her day of judgment wasn't bad enough, knowing that Blake wouldn't be there to soothe her worries made it a hundred times worse.

For the millionth time since their fight, her heart crumpled. All the guitar playing in the world wouldn't ease what ailed her. She'd spent the first few days in abject misery, until she'd grown so tired of being miserable she'd finally pulled herself together and thrown her energies into her plans for the club.

Assuming, of course, that Sara got the charges against her dropped so she could get her old job back.

The elevator finally arrived with a ping, and Jax entered, pushing the button for the correct floor. Amazingly enough, the thought of losing her job no longer sent her into a fit of panic. It hadn't taken long for her to realize that she would trade it all in if Blake loved her enough, trusted in her enough to let go of the stupid fear that held him in its grip. But he didn't trust her judgment, not with the decisions she made about her life...or as the mother of his baby.

The crushing truth pinned her heart painfully, but she pushed the thoughts aside as the doors opened and she exited the elevator. Now was not the time to dwell on what could have been. Her baby was depending on her, and Jax had a date with a judge....

With a hard swallow, she gripped her tote tightly as she hurried down the hall. Nerves and baby butterflies knocked in her stomach as Jax pushed through the door to the courtroom, braced for the chastising glares. Or perhaps reprimanding words of warning. She just prayed the bailiff wasn't waiting to clap her in handcuffs and haul her away. But she was shocked to discover the staff hovered around a computer monitor, completely unconcerned the accused had arrived late.

She stopped short, adjusting to the fact that her expectations for disaster had morphed into a nonevent.

"Jax," a female voice blurted, and she turned to see Nikki and Abigail—along with several of the kids and staff from the club—waving as they sat at one of the benches that lined the courtroom like pews in a church. Which seemed fitting, seeing how her prayers had just been answered.

Too bad the one that really mattered hadn't come true.

The encouraging smiles of her friends and makeshift family, along with Abigail's two-thumbs-up gesture, were so welcome that a sting of grateful tears threatened. Jax swallowed them back and waved in return.

Hoping to take a seat before her late arrival was noticed, she turned and hurried up the aisle toward the front of the room. And then she spied the back of a familiar dark-headed figure clad in a gorgeous suit, and her stomach stopped, dropped and rolled to her toes.

Her footsteps slowed, and when Blake turned in his seat and met her gaze, she spent the next five seconds trying to pry her heart from her throat.

The look he shot her was loaded. And as his eyes roamed over her with a mixture of relief, elation and hunger, her body thrummed in response. His desire was a given, but was he glad to see *her*? Or was he just glad she looked well because he was worried about his baby? Maybe he was just grateful the mother of his child might avoid a conviction now that she'd finally shown up.

Heart tapping out a rhythm so fast she was sure the beat could be felt across the courtroom, she adopted the coolest, most unflustered look she could and slid into the seat next to Blake.

"I'm late," she whispered stupidly, because it sure beat weeping and throwing herself into his arms like the emotional, hormonal woman she was. And the only other option was to punch him on the arm and tell him to start dealing with his father's death in a constructive way. "I couldn't find a parking spot."

"No worries," he whispered back. "There was a bit of a delay so no one's noticed."

"Where's Sara?"

"I paid her generously for her time and told her I'd take care of today."

Despite her twenty-three years of practice, breathing suddenly became a complicated process. "Please tell me you aren't planning on losing my case so I don't get hired back at the club."

His gaze firm, he oozed confidence. "I plan on getting every charge against you dropped."

She blinked hard. "Oh," she said, feeling even more stupid for suggesting he'd intentionally sabotage her future. Of course he wouldn't want her convicted of a crime. She was carrying his child. "Well…" She struggled to swallow past her tight throat. "Thank you."

His gray eyes held her captive, so cool juxtaposed against the handsome planes of his face and dark eyebrows, one bisected by that tiny yet very significant scar. Given all they'd been through, her thanks had sounded weak and anemic, and a flush of embarrassingly awkward heat infused her face. The bustling of the courtroom staff sounded far away. Reflexively she laid her hand on her abdomen, gathering strength from the adorable little imp currently wreaking havoc in her belly, wishing she could allow herself to hope for something more.

"Will you marry me?" he said in a low voice, startling her with the words.

The burning threat of tears was instantaneous, and she was grateful the threat never materialized. It would be hard to hold an intelligent conversation while crying like a silly baby. Because her heart longed for her to scream yes. But sometimes blindly following her heart wasn't the wise thing to do.

Sometimes the future, your *best* future, depended on remaining rational. Logical. And this was definitely one of those times.

Although she whispered, her voice was strong. "I love you, Blake," she said, the words so heartfelt they hurt coming out. "And maybe I *am* a little overly sensitive about my past. But I deserve better than a man who is constantly questioning my judgment." Blake grimaced and sucked in a breath, regret radiating in his expression. But a simple "I'm sorry" or an "I messed up" wasn't going to cut it. Their life together, their family, was too important for her to give in so easily. She forced herself to continue to meet his gaze, refusing to concede too soon, and she straightened her shoulders for good measure. "And I can't live with a man who is marrying me only out of a sense of duty and responsibility."

Several heartbeats passed as Jax braced for the speech she was sure he'd prepared. With his years of practice swaying juries, no doubt it was going to be a doozy.

Warrior, Jax. Remember, you are a warrior.

"I'm not asking you because of the baby," he said in a low voice, his jaw set, emotion brimming in his eyes. "And I'm not asking you because being with you makes me happy, or because I see your scars as a sign of your incredible strength. I'm not even asking because your amazing courage has inspired me to give up a promotion that would have made me miserable."

Her voice came out with a surprised squeak. "You're passing up the promotion?"

"I'm passing up the promotion."

Her heart softened a touch, and his eyes caressed her face. With effort, she steadfastly ignored the muscular body encased in a beautiful suit as she breathed in his fresh, sea-breeze scent. The familiar thrum of awareness returned, and the pounding in her chest cranked higher as he went on.

"I'm not even worried about the fact that Nikki and my mother will kill me for permanently blowing my chances with you," he said as he shot her a helpless grin.

Her heart turned over in her chest, and she suppressed the need to return the smile. At least his prepared speech was living up to her expectations.

He leaned in, and the intensity in his eyes and his proximity left her spinning, her body sighing happily at having him close again as he went on. "I'm asking you to marry me because I've fallen in love with you and I can't imagine any other woman being more perfect for me than you."

Heart hammering louder in her ears, Jax feared she was

beginning to lose the war with her encroaching tears, her heart mushier than ever before.

He loved her.

Hope gaining a huge foothold, Jax tried for a chastising tone, but barely even convinced herself. "You picked a fine time for your confession, Suit." She sent him a watery smile and sniffed, lifting a brow. "But don't you want to wait until the outcome of my trial before you make the marriage commitment?"

"Convicted criminal or not," he said, his voice strong, "you are the woman for me."

She forced back the surge of tears. "That's the most romantic thing I've ever heard."

Hope flared in Blake's eyes. "Jax, please marry—"

"Okay, folks," the clerk said from the front of the room, and Jax bit back the scream of frustration. "Technical malfunction fixed. Though we hardly needed the IT crew." The man scratched his balding head, clearly perplexed. "Somehow the computer cable got pulled from the network card."

Surprise shot through her, and Jax whipped her head around to look at Blake—the man who was now leaning back in his chair with an expression akin to the cat that had swallowed the canary. A very *delicious* canary. Jax recognized the faint glimmer of amusement in his eyes, and her stomach did a slow-motion flip as the reason for the delay finally sank in.

Eyes wide with disbelief, she leaned in close to Blake. "Did you pull the plug to buy me time to get here?" she whispered.

His brow instantly crinkled with humor. "Certainly not," he said smoothly. "Because that would be wrong."

But the light in his eyes suggested otherwise.

She blinked hard once, trying to adjust. How he'd pulled off his little stunt without anyone noticing, she had no idea. But after years of being the man who ensured society followed the letter of the law, obeyed every rule in the rulebook, the hell-raiser Blake had briefly made a reappearance.

All in an effort to ensure Jax's tardiness would go unnoticed.

And with that, every defense she had left in her arsenal drained away. Her heart melted, pooled at her feet and spread far and wide. Coating her world with hope.

Impressed, and terribly, terribly touched, all she could do was stare at Blake. And when the clerk announced that it was time to begin, she was still so powerfully affected that Blake had to pull her to her feet when Judge Conner entered the courtroom.

The trial seemed to drag by in slow motion, but through sheer strength of will, Blake focused all his efforts on the proceedings. But it wasn't easy with Jax beside him, smelling of apples spiced with cinnamon. Her red blouse brought out the honey coloring of her wild, tumbling hair, and the denim skirt was long enough to be respectable—but with enough bared leg to be a major distraction.

The return of those sexy cowboy boots wasn't helping, either.

And when the verdict came to drop all the charges against Jax, Blake let out a long, slow, satisfied breath. Jax turned to him, her eyes bright, her lovely face glowing, and it took every ounce of self-control he had not to claim her delectable mouth in a kiss. To ease the gnawing ache her absence had brought.

Because he needed this bold, courageous woman in his life.

"Now, Ms. Lee," Judge Connor said, his demeanor, as always, staid, "let's see that you steer clear of even the appearance of trouble from here on out. And as for your opinion of the Ramones…" The older man's eyes twinkled as he nodded in the direction of Jax's tote on the table, the band's logo clearly displayed on the side. "You're wrong. The Clash and the Sex Pistols were much more influential."

Spying Jax's suspiciously innocuous expression, Blake tensed.

But her smile was surprisingly submissive. "Yes, sir."

He exhaled in a quiet whoosh, and, as the courtroom began to disband, Jax shot Blake a defiantly innocent look.

"What?" she said, as if she'd seen his concern. "Did you think I was going to argue with the judge?"

"Not in the slightest," he lied, biting back a smile.

He loved how Jax rushed in where practical people feared to tread. Because it was her courage and her heart and her zest for life that he needed the most. And one thing was for certain—a life with Jacqueline Lee would always be exciting.

That was, of course, if he could get her to agree to marry him.

His gut churned with an anxiety that had been eating at him since he'd blown his first proposal. Forging ahead with the proceeding with the woman he loved beside him—*still* not knowing whether she'd marry him or not—was one of the hardest things he'd ever done. And if he didn't hear an answer to his proposal soon, he was going to crack under the pressure.

Which meant he needed to get her alone.

Blake grabbed his briefcase and took Jax's elbow, steering her toward the exit, hoping to slip out the door unnoticed. "Jax," he began, his pulse pounding, "I—"

"I told you Blake was a brilliant lawyer," a castless Nikki said as she appeared in front of them. Blake tamped down the disappointment and waited patiently as his grinning sister gave Jax a brief hug. And then Nikki turned to Blake with a huge smile. "You were awesome, big brother," she said with a hug for him, too, infusing a warm feeling through his limbs.

But Blake hoped to hurry this process along. "Thank y—"

"Almost as awesome as his mother," his mom said as she

emerged to envelope Jax in a tight embrace, looking as if she'd never let her go.

And with the irksome upgrade of their three's-a-crowd status to four, Blake met Jax's amused eyes over his mother's shoulders. Clearly, she could sense his frustration. Or maybe she was just relieved because she wanted to put off his proposal again. Maybe she could never forgive him for his cowardly behavior.

His apprehension climbed to seriously uncomfortable levels, and, desperate to get an answer, he ushered the band of females toward the exit.

Nikki leaned in close and whispered, "Did she say yes?"

Lungs tight with fear, he whispered back, "I can't get her alone long enough to find out."

Unfortunately, the situation got worse when they entered the hallway, and Blake's heart sank. The waiting crowd was large, Jax's colleagues and a quite a few teens from the club swarming around her. Obviously excited, Jax stopped to hug each one in turn as Blake fought to keep his dismay from showing.

He shot his sister a desperate look, and she smiled slyly in understanding.

When an empty elevator opened before them, Blake firmly took Jax's arm and led her inside. And Nikki turned and blocked anyone else from entering.

Man, there was nothing better than being blessed with a wonderfully reckless sister.

"Listen up, everybody," Nikki said with an authority that did him proud. "I'm moving this celebratory party to my brother's house." Blake ignored the concern her words brought as she went on. "But right now Blake needs to discuss a few lingering legal issues with Jax."

And then Nikki stepped away from the elevator and turned, shooting Blake a wink before the door closed and cut off the view of her mischievous expression.

Alone at last, the silence weighed heavily, and as the elevator descended, the tension in his muscles climbed. "Jax," he said, scanning the beautiful hazel eyes and forcing himself to ignore the smooth expanse of legs, "I—"

"How did you distract the courtroom staff when you pulled the computer cord?"

He let out a disbelieving scoff and shoved a hand through his hair, struggling for composure. His stunt wasn't the topic he wanted to discuss. He certainly didn't want to remember how, after asking *Nikki* for help, his mother had taken over and pretended to faint.

And she had milked her dramatic ruse for all it was worth until someone suggested dialing 911.

The doors slid open, and they stepped out into the lobby. Escorting her toward the exit, Blake took her arm again. But it was just an excuse to touch her.

"I told you," he answered smoothly, his brow bunching with suppressed humor. "I'd never pull a stunt like that. Except, maybe—" he shot her a hopeful look from the corner of his eye "—to help the woman I love."

Discouraged by her continued silence, Blake followed Jax through the front door and out into the bright sunshine, and she paused at the top of the courthouse steps to look up at him, her expression thoughtful. He stepped close, seeking comfort in her scent and aching for the woman who'd brought him back to life.

Desperate to be the lucky man who occasionally got to bail her out of trouble.

With an amused smile, Jax gazed up at him, studying him with an emotion he couldn't interpret. "And how did it feel to break the rules?"

Blake hesitated. Ten years of tension—of striving daily to live up to his promises to his father—had taken a toll on his spirit. But fusing lust and need back with logic and reason was the only way to heal his soul. Jax had known that, and he knew his father would have approved, too.

His brow crinkled in amusement. "It felt good."

Jax tugged on his tie and pulled him closer, not stopping until they were toe-to-toe. And when her soft body was pressed against his, desire and love and a hope for happiness hit him all at once. With an expectant face, she waited for him to go on, plainly enjoying making him work for her answer.

"I can't think of anyone more qualified to raise the next generation of Benningtons," he said truthfully. "Who else will be able to handle my family? My mother's baked goods?" His lips twisted wryly. "Not to mention coolly redirect my mixed-up craziness when I freak out?"

"Like when our son gets his driver's license?"

There was no suppressing his groan of fear.

"Or when our daughter moves into a coed dorm at college?" she added.

A muttered curse escaped his mouth, and he didn't bother replying to the petrifying idea.

Instead, he slid his palm to her abdomen, splaying his fingers across her belly and the scars beneath. Touching the bleak teenage years of her past and the beautiful baby in their future. Her gaze smoldered in response, and need kicked him with a vengeance.

His words gruff, he said, "I think it's in the best interests of our baby that you marry me and keep a close eye on my erratic behavior."

Her return smile was the most beautiful thing he'd ever seen. "I think you're right."

With a groan of relief, he claimed her mouth for a kiss. And as the bright sun heated them from overhead, he savored her wild flavor, the reckless response of her lips and the damp heat of her sweet mouth. When she tasted his tongue with hers, desire skewered him, and he gripped her hips.

But Jax pulled her mouth away, her eyes shining up at him. "What were you going to do if I had said no?"

His heart still pounding with love and lust, he quirked his lips in humor. "You mean after I freaked out?" Jax let out a laugh and he went on. "Nikki and I asked several of your teens to do a flash-mob singing proposal for me when we arrived on the courthouse lawn," he said. "Carefully following the letter of the law, of course."

Her lids slowly stretched wide, her eyes sparkling. "Really? A singing proposal?" she said, obviously charmed by the idea. She looked around, and when the courthouse green clearly held no youth preparing to belt out a tune, her face fell a touch. "Now I'm kinda sorry I said yes already."

He shot her a scorching look. "So I'll take you home and make you glad you did."

Her breath caught, and her voice sounded winded. "But Nikki moved our audience back to your house to celebrate."

"Then we'll sneak back to the guesthouse while they start the celebration without us."

She pulled back a touch, raising an eyebrow. "You really are turning back into a hell-raiser."

Blake pulled her closer, savoring his amazing good fortune. "Only around you, Jax," he murmured, heading in for another kiss. "Only around you."

* * * * *

Mills & Boon® Hardback
March 2013

ROMANCE

Playing the Dutiful Wife	Carol Marinelli
The Fallen Greek Bride	Jane Porter
A Scandal, a Secret, a Baby	Sharon Kendrick
The Notorious Gabriel Diaz	Cathy Williams
A Reputation For Revenge	Jennie Lucas
Captive in the Spotlight	Annie West
Taming the Last Acosta	Susan Stephens
Island of Secrets	Robyn Donald
The Taming of a Wild Child	Kimberly Lang
First Time For Everything	Aimee Carson
Guardian to the Heiress	Margaret Way
Little Cowgirl on His Doorstep	Donna Alward
Mission: Soldier to Daddy	Soraya Lane
Winning Back His Wife	Melissa McClone
The Guy To Be Seen With	Fiona Harper
Why Resist a Rebel?	Leah Ashton
Sydney Harbour Hospital: Evie's Bombshell	Amy Andrews
The Prince Who Charmed Her	Fiona McArthur

MEDICAL

NYC Angels: Redeeming The Playboy	Carol Marinelli
NYC Angels: Heiress's Baby Scandal	Janice Lynn
St Piran's: The Wedding!	Alison Roberts
His Hidden American Beauty	Connie Cox

Mills & Boon® Large Print

March 2013

ROMANCE

A Night of No Return	Sarah Morgan
A Tempestuous Temptation	Cathy Williams
Back in the Headlines	Sharon Kendrick
A Taste of the Untamed	Susan Stephens
The Count's Christmas Baby	Rebecca Winters
His Larkville Cinderella	Melissa McClone
The Nanny Who Saved Christmas	Michelle Douglas
Snowed in at the Ranch	Cara Colter
Exquisite Revenge	Abby Green
Beneath the Veil of Paradise	Kate Hewitt
Surrendering All But Her Heart	Melanie Milburne

HISTORICAL

How to Sin Successfully	Bronwyn Scott
Hattie Wilkinson Meets Her Match	Michelle Styles
The Captain's Kidnapped Beauty	Mary Nichols
The Admiral's Penniless Bride	Carla Kelly
Return of the Border Warrior	Blythe Gifford

MEDICAL

Her Motherhood Wish	Anne Fraser
A Bond Between Strangers	Scarlet Wilson
Once a Playboy…	Kate Hardy
Challenging the Nurse's Rules	Janice Lynn
The Sheikh and the Surrogate Mum	Meredith Webber
Tamed by her Brooding Boss	Joanna Neil

0213 GEN STD LP

Mills & Boon® Hardback

April 2013

ROMANCE

Master of her Virtue	Miranda Lee
The Cost of her Innocence	Jacqueline Baird
A Taste of the Forbidden	Carole Mortimer
Count Valieri's Prisoner	Sara Craven
The Merciless Travis Wilde	Sandra Marton
A Game with One Winner	Lynn Raye Harris
Heir to a Desert Legacy	Maisey Yates
The Sinful Art of Revenge	Maya Blake
Marriage in Name Only?	Anne Oliver
Waking Up Married	Mira Lyn Kelly
Sparks Fly with the Billionaire	Marion Lennox
A Daddy for Her Sons	Raye Morgan
Along Came Twins…	Rebecca Winters
An Accidental Family	Ami Weaver
A Date with a Bollywood Star	Riya Lakhani
The Proposal Plan	Charlotte Phillips
Their Most Forbidden Fling	Melanie Milburne
The Last Doctor She Should Ever Date	Louisa George

MEDICAL

NYC Angels: Unmasking Dr Serious	Laura Iding
NYC Angels: The Wallflower's Secret	Susan Carlisle
Cinderella of Harley Street	Anne Fraser
You, Me and a Family	Sue MacKay

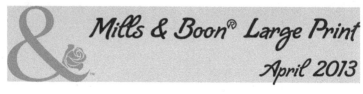
Mills & Boon® Large Print

April 2013

ROMANCE

A Ring to Secure His Heir	Lynne Graham
What His Money Can't Hide	Maggie Cox
Woman in a Sheikh's World	Sarah Morgan
At Dante's Service	Chantelle Shaw
The English Lord's Secret Son	Margaret Way
The Secret That Changed Everything	Lucy Gordon
The Cattleman's Special Delivery	Barbara Hannay
Her Man in Manhattan	Trish Wylie
At His Majesty's Request	Maisey Yates
Breaking the Greek's Rules	Anne McAllister
The Ruthless Caleb Wilde	Sandra Marton

HISTORICAL

Some Like It Wicked	Carole Mortimer
Born to Scandal	Diane Gaston
Beneath the Major's Scars	Sarah Mallory
Warriors in Winter	Michelle Willingham
A Stranger's Touch	Anne Herries

MEDICAL

A Socialite's Christmas Wish	Lucy Clark
Redeeming Dr Riccardi	Leah Martyn
The Family Who Made Him Whole	Jennifer Taylor
The Doctor Meets Her Match	Annie Claydon
The Doctor's Lost-and-Found Heart	Dianne Drake
The Man Who Wouldn't Marry	Tina Beckett

0313 GEN STD LP

Discover Pure Reading Pleasure with

Visit the Mills & Boon website for all the latest in romance

 Buy all the latest releases, backlist and eBooks

 Find out more about our authors and their books

 Join our community and chat to authors and other readers

 Free online reads from your favourite authors

 Win with our fantastic online competitions

 Sign up for our free monthly eNewsletter

 Tell us what you think by signing up to our reader panel

 Rate and review books with our star system

www.millsandboon.co.uk

 Follow us at twitter.com/millsandboonuk

 Become a fan at facebook.com/romancehq